To Shei~
Happy
Hugs, ~uks
Barbara + Luna

WHO
RESCUED
WHO 2?

MORE Tales of Street Dogs
and the People Who Love Them

Barbara Harkness
& Valerie Siegel

Published by StreetDogs Press

© Copyright October 2013
Barbara Harkness; Valerie Siegel
ISBN: 978-0-9884495-2-7
Printed in Mexico

Design: Mike Riley, www.ajijicbooks.com

Other books by the authors:
*Who Rescued Who: Tales of Street Dogs and
the People Who Love Them* © 2012

To Luna and Winston

…you inspire us, you surprise and delight us… every day.
And we aspire to be the huMoms you believe we are.

Who Rescued Who?

It came to me that every time I lose a dog, they take a piece of my heart with them.

And every new dog who comes into my life gifts me with a piece of its heart.

If I live long enough, all the components of my heart will be dog, and maybe I will become as generous and loving as they are.

Author unknown

Getting Acquainted

Many of these tales take place in an enchanted part of interior Mexico. Some of the locations and terms may be unfamiliar to you. This will help you get familiar.

- ❖ Abarrotero (ah-bah-row-ter-ro) = corner grocery store.
- ❖ Ajijic (ah-hee-heek) = a village located on the north shore of Lake Chapala, west of the town of Chapala.
- ❖ Amigo (ah-mee-go) = male friend.
- ❖ Anita's = Anita's Animals is a shelter for dogs in the San Juan Cosala area.
- ❖ Arroyo (ah-roy-oh) = river.
- ❖ Baja California Sud = the southern end (sud) of the Mexican state of Baja California, located on the peninsula south of the US state of California.
- ❖ Barrio (bar-ee-oh) = neighborhood.
- ❖ Bebe (bay-bay) = baby.
- ❖ Buenos dias (bway-nos dee-ass) = good morning
- ❖ Carpinteria (car-peen-tar-ee-ah) = a business that does woodworking.
- ❖ Carretera (cah-rah-terr-ah) = main road, highway.
- ❖ Chapalino (Chap-ah-lee-no) = slang term for a resident of Chapala.
- ❖ Chilango (Chee-lan-go) = slang term for a resident of Mexico City.
- ❖ Cohetes (ko-et-ays) = rockets used to celebrate special occasions.
- ❖ Comida (co-mee-dah) = mid-day meal, eaten around 2 pm.
- ❖ Comprende (com-pren-day)= understand.
- ❖ Gata (gah-tah) = female cat.
- ❖ Gordo (gor-doh) = chubby.
- ❖ Gringa (green-gah) = a female native speaker of English.
- ❖ Habla usted español = do you speak Spanish?
- ❖ Hola = hi.

Who Rescued Who 2?

- ❖ Ixtlahuacan de los Membrillos (eeks-tla-whah-kan day los mehm-bree-yohs) = a town located 18 miles south of Guadalajara and 12 miles north of Lake Chapala.
- ❖ Jocotepec (ho-ko-teh-pec) = a village located on the north shore and the west end of Lake Chapala.
- ❖ Malecon (mah-lay-con) = boardwalk along the lakeshore.
- ❖ Nahuatl (Na-hwa-tal) = a group of native Aztec languages spoken mostly in central Mexico.
- ❖ Ocotlan (oh-coat-lan) = a village located northeast of Lake Chapala.
- ❖ Papacito (pah-pah-see-toh)= affectionate term for father.
- ❖ Pemex (peh-mex) = national gas station of Mexico.
- ❖ Perrito (pair-ee-toh) = small dog.
- ❖ Pobrecita (poh-bray-see-tah) = poor little thing.
- ❖ Por que (por kay) = why.
- ❖ Privada (pree-vah-dah) = dead-end street.
- ❖ Riberas/Riberas del Pilar (ree-bear-ahs del pee-lar) = a village located on the north shore of Lake Chapala between Ajijic and Chapala.
- ❖ San Antonio Tlayacapan = a village located on the north shore of Lake Chapala, adjacent to and east of the village of Ajijic.
- ❖ Santa Cruz de la Soledad = a village located on the north shore of Lake Chapala, east of the town of Chapala.
- ❖ Sra = señora (sen-youra) term of respect for a woman.
- ❖ Te quiero mucho (Tay kee-ay-roh mooch-oh) = I love you very much.
- ❖ Tia (tee-ah) = aunt.
- ❖ Tianguis (tee-an-gees) = weekly, open air street market.
- ❖ Zaragoza Prolongacion = a street in Chapala.

… and now you know.

Tributes...

By the edge of a woods, at the foot of a hill,
Is a lush, green meadow where time stands still.
Where the friends of man and woman do run,
When their time on earth is over and done.

For here, between this world and the next,
Is a place where each beloved creature finds rest.
On this golden land, they wait and they play,
Till the Rainbow Bridge they cross over one day.

No more do they suffer, in pain or in sadness,
For here they are whole, their lives filled with gladness.
Their limbs are restored, their health renewed,
Their bodies have healed, with strength imbued.

They romp through the grass, without even a care,
Until one day they start, and sniff at the air.
All ears prick forward, eyes dart front and back,
Then all of a sudden, one breaks from the pack.

For just at that instant, their eyes have met;
Together again, both person and pet.
So they run to each other, these friends from long past,
The time of their parting is over at last.

The sadness they felt while they were apart,
Has turned into joy once more in each heart.
They embrace with a love that will last forever,
And then, side-by-side, they cross over... together.

Rainbow Bridge
By Steve and Diane Bodofsky

Te Quiero Mucho

Nettie was thirteen years old and solidly in the grip of anorexia nervosa. Her parents, desperate for help, had consulted with psychiatrists, other medical doctors and behaviorists. Finally, someone suggested that the best medicine for a young girl is a puppy. "As she takes care of the puppy, she will take care of herself." The advice sounded reasonable to parents desperate to help their child before it was too late.

Yves and his wife, whose name is also Nettie, learned of a person some distance from their home who was giving away American Cocker Spaniels. They would have to hurry because there was only one left. At the end of the long drive, made longer by getting lost in an unfamiliar area, they found a tiny, wiggly cotton-ball only three months old. At once, they named her Peque, which means small.

On her first night home, Peque slept between mother and daughter. In the morning, while exploring the surface of her new fur ball, young Nettie found hard black bumps against the skin. She had never seen such things on an animal. Ticks! That launched young Nettie into the care of her tiny furry friend that continued for ten years.

As a puppy, Peque was full of mischief. The family lived on a large family property where there were three houses. One day when she was out of Nettie's sight, Peque left her own house and went to the home of a family member who had brought home a luscious kilo of barbecued ribs for lunch. Peque accepted a luncheon invitation that, well, was not actually extended to her. Nettie rescued her barbecue-drenched puppy in the nick of time from a most disgruntled uncle.

Together Nettie and Peque grew to enjoy good health and a happy life. Once Peque came into her care, Nettie was symptom free. When she finally married ten years later, Nettie moved for her husband's job to a place where dogs were unwelcome. Peque remained behind with Nettie's parents, living the next eight years in Nettie's heart.

I will always love you, Nettie.

Peque crossed the Rainbow Bridge in January 2013. Nettie's words followed her:

> Peque was an angel who came into my life at a very difficult moment. We became companions for life. Today she leaves this earth to guide us from heaven. Seventeen years of life started to show in her fatigue. Her heart stopped today. I will miss you like never before and I want to thank you for every moment you gave me.
>
> Te quiero mucho.

Footprints on Her Heart

She was born in 1918 In Portland, Indiana. She never joined a march for a cause. She never organized a demonstration to make a point.

She got her pilot's license and was qualified to fly across the country. She got some of her training on a Beech AT-10 aircraft. She's a graduate of the University of Indiana in Indianapolis. She was married and divorced… twice. She was a newspaper reporter, a school secretary, a wife and a mother. She loves music and plays the piano… a little less these days. She's small of stature with a huge personality.

Jeannette Saylor lives her life as an example to her four children… all of whom have accomplished excellence in their careers. Susie… a nurse with a biochemistry degree and a classical concert pianist; Cindy… an advertising executive, professional singer and producer; Joe… a professional contemporary jazz composer, performer and piano tuner; and Steven… a rocket scientist with Boeing, a guitarist and biker.

Music is an important theme in all of their lives… because of Jeannette. She constantly played jazz records and insisted they all have music lessons. They were the midwest version of the Von Trapp family (Sound of Music), Susie would play Funiculi, Funicula on the piano… her sister and brothers would gather round and sing. Cindy and Susie learned how to sing harmony while doing the dishes.

Those four children are the great loves of Jeannette's life. A smile spreads across her face and her eyes light up when she proudly talks about them and their achievements.

Another love of her life was like one of her children. It was a very special, glossy auburn-haired Cocker Spaniel, with freckles on his face… a gift from her brother-in-law. She named him AT-10, AT for short, for her favorite aircraft. He went everywhere with her. He loved and adored her as much as she loved and adored him.

Susie, Jeannette's eldest daughter, grew up with AT. They were pals and "only" children for five years. AT was just as indulged as Susie. The day Jeannette brought her newborn, Cindy, home from the hospital, AT moped around while everyone admired the new baby. He ran and hid under the bed... and would not come out. Everyone tried to coax him. Jeannette took a bone and lured him out. He moved slowly with the saddest eyes she had ever seen. Every time she sat on a chair, he would jump into her lap, wanting her attention. He finally adjusted to the new being in the house.

AT loved the car. On family outings, he would sit proudly in Jeannette's lap, just looking around at the scenery. He never asked, "Are we there yet?" because he enjoyed being close to Jeannette so much.

Their home was a haven for all sorts of animals... cats, birds, and fish... whatever seemed to need a place to live, even temporarily. AT took a particular liking to some kittens. He thought they were toys. One day Jeannette caught him playing a bit too roughly with them. She hollered at him. He looked chastised... and never did it again.

Life was different in the 1940s and 50s... there was more freedom and a greater sense of safety than today. AT never had to be walked on a leash. He had the freedom of the neighborhood. Everyone knew him and loved him.

A girl of about 16, who lived in the neighborhood, was passing Jeannette on the street one day and shoved past her... literally shoved her. AT immediately reacted... growling and baring his teeth, he went for the girl. Jeannette intervened before anything happened.

A couple of days later, AT was out wandering the neighborhood as he often did. He ate something that had been left out on a porch. The neighbors did that a lot. AT took care of leftovers for them. Not feeling well, he returned home to lie in the coolness under the porch... which he rarely did. His normal resting position was in front of the door to guard against anyone going into the house, unauthorized.

Jeannette returned home from doing errands and did not see

AT in his usual spot. She called for him... once... twice... and then she heard a whimpering from under the porch. She ran over, called AT's name and could tell the dog was very sick. He could barely move and had foam around his mouth. Jeannette reached in and gently pulled him out to her and cradled him in her arms. She remembers letting out a scream of "Nooooooooooooooooooooo" as AT took his last breath.

She describes it as one of the worst days of her life.

After 16 years of loyalty, companionship and affection, AT was buried under some "mourning" glories on the north side of the yard. Jeannette vowed she would never have another dog in her life. It would be just too painful.

Small in stature with a *huge* personality

I Love You, Jeannette

In 1942 the world was in the middle of a war. Franklin D. Roosevelt was the President of the United States. I think Elmer R. Corn was the mayor of Wichita, Kansas, where I lived.

The St. Louis Cardinals were World Series Champions. Humans were going to the movies to see Casablanca and to ogle Gene Tierney, Rita Hayworth, Lana Turner and Betty Grable.

If you could buy a new car, it would cost about $920 and 15 cents a gallon to fill the gas tank. We had a car.

I lived in a house where we listened to music on the radio a lot… most of the guys had funny sounding names, like Duke Ellington, Dizzy Gillespie, Hoagy Carmichael and Thelonious Monk. The ladies had some killer-diller voices… Ooooooooooh that Lena Horne… and Peggy Lee. My favorite human, Jeannette, played the piano. I loooooooooooved to listen to her. I could lay down by that piano for hours just dozing and listening to her tickle those ivories.

We had a big yard in a great neighborhood. It was a gas running all over the place and visiting people. We had a victory garden where Jeannette grew vegetables and then she put some in cans and jars and kept them to eat later. She was busy. She washed clothes and things on the porch… in a basin and with a hand cranked wringer machine. Then she pinned the stuff on a line for the sun and the wind to dry it.

When I came to live with Jeannette, she had a little human called Susie. At first Susie didn't do much except eat and sleep. For a while she crawled on the grass and I ran around her and barked and sniffed and licked her. When she started walking, we really had fun.

At night time, before we went to sleep, Jeannette read to us from these Little Golden Books. My favorite story was Bambi. It was about a baby deer, maybe you know it?

One day, Jeannette brought home a bundle that she held in her arms. All the humans were smiling and looking at the bundle. Even Susie was jumping up and down shouting, "I want to see the baby… I want to see the baby." No one petted me. Jeannette didn't even look at me. I went and hid under the bed. If they don't want to see me, then I don't want to see them. Humans came and talked at me. I just ignored them. I was sulking.

Then Jeanette came to talk to me in that voice I loved. She had my favorite kind of bone. So I came out slowly and looked at her with my most pathetic expression. I wanted her to know how hurt I felt… and maybe a little jealous of that new bundle. They called her Cindy.

After a while, things got back to normal. I could jump on Jeannette's lap for a snuggle… when that Cindy wasn't there. When she grew up and started crawling and walking, I got more time with my Jeannette.

I love you, Jeanette

She and I would go walking to see neighbors. She would walk the girls in these chairs with wheels. On our way home one day a girl shoved Jeannette, really hard. She almost fell over. Well, I growled at that girl and showed her my teeth and started toward her to let her know she better not mess with me. Jeannette grabbed me and I calmed down. The girl muttered something not nice and ran away.

I was out on my rounds one morning… just running around

saying hi-de-ho to the neighbor ladies and eating up the bowls they left out for me. I think it might have been right after I ate at the house that nasty girl lived in that I started to feel funny. My stomach was making funny noises. I was thirsty. I got sick. I had to get home.

I ran under the porch because it looked like a cool spot and I was feeling verrrrry warm… and thirsty… and foamy stuff was in my mouth. I felt like I couldn't breathe. I heard my Jeannette call my name. I had to get to her. She would make me better. I crawled out. She held me in her arms. She was rocking me and crying.

The last thing I remember hearing was Jeanette's voice screaming, "Noooooooooooooooooooooo."

I crossed over the Rainbow Bridge without having the chance to say good-bye to my Jeannette and my family. I didn't have the opportunity to tell her how much I loved her and what a great life I had with them. I'm still waiting for her… so one day I can lick her face again and tell her, "I love you, Jeannette."

El Campeón

When the symptoms first began she had been a Mexican national living in Berlin where she worked for a major pharmaceutical company. Extreme pain. Chronic. No diagnosis. As time went on, the consensus among the physicians she consulted was that her pain was stress related. Two years would pass before a diagnosis of fibromyalgia was finally offered. The diagnosis did nothing to alleviate the pain.

Sleep deprived and desperate for pain relief, she began to explore ways to end her life. She contacted an organization in Europe that sent her information. She learned how to do what she needed to do. She also learned she did not fit their protocol for assisted suicide. Constant, unbearable pain alone was insufficient for acceptance into their program and without acceptance, she could not get the substance required to end her life.

She returned to Mexico where she felt certain she could find what she needed. By now the pain was so excruciating that getting out of bed was, on some days, all she could manage. She settled in a picturesque little village woven with cobblestone streets and colorful shops, and drenched in sunlight. With time and determination, she was able to locate the substance she needed. She learned she could get it in sufficient quantity to stop the pain forever.

She was able to get out of bed and dress herself the next morning and prepared to travel to Guadalajara to make the necessary purchase. When she opened her front door, her eyes fell upon a big strong-looking, light beige Pit Bull mix dog. His stance was tough as he looked up at her with soulful brown eyes. Over the next four months, she would come to recognize his sad expression as the only one he ever wore.

He was sitting directly in front of her door. She could not get around him and he did not move. He just looked at her. And she looked at him. In her fatigue, her pain, and her disbelief that this creature showed up on her doorstep at this moment, she retreated into her little house.

In the weeks that followed, she named him El Campeón because he was her champ. He was battle-scarred and wary, and he stood as a sentry in front of her tiny house for days. Her purpose in life became his care. She had to feed him, to give him water, and to make a home for him.

El Campeón would have none of the homemaking. He scratched at the doors, threw himself against the windows, and ripped up the furniture. The final straw was her attempt to leash train him. He bolted. For a week.

As she grew more concerned about her El Campeón, her pain dissipated. Shifting her concern from her own condition to his welfare energized her. She became very aware of his aggression as he protected her home, and was concerned that he might one day lose a fight. The scars he bore told her he had survived many.

Within a few months she was totally focused on finding a home for him with someone who knew how to socialize him. The possible alternatives were unacceptable to her. As she understood them, they were being caged for life in a no-kill shelter, or euthanized in a kill policy shelter.

After the four months she and her El Campeón had been together, she felt frightened when he disappeared from the front of her house. She searched her small village for three days until some construction workers took her to what they believed to be her dog.

And it was. El Campeón was lying peacefully on the ground in an empty lot not far from the home he had protected and the life inside it that he had saved. His path to the Rainbow Bridge is unknown even as his legacy continues to unfold.

Animal regulations in the village where El Campeón lived are among the most stringent in the state of Jalisco. The woman whose life he saved has become a full-time activist who has worked successfully to pass animal welfare legislation all over Mexico. Because of her work, several Mexican jurisdictions have banned bullfighting. And legislation is pending in others to do the same.

She is currently facilitating an educational program in 51 schools in Jalisco, the purpose of which is to decrease violent behavior and to teach respect for all living beings. She says, "I owe my life, my improving health, and my work to El Campeón."

I Chose Her

In the beginning, I wasn't chosen. My three brothers and one sister were chosen. I wasn't chosen. I lived for a long time in the place where I was born. I slept outside in the dirt. I had plenty to eat and water to drink. It never rained where I lived. In the cool of the morning, I was let off my chain to run. Like all puppies, I loved to run. And I always came back because that's where the food and water were. Where I lived, even the humans were without much of either.

I don't remember how old I was when humans...always male humans...came to look at me. Again, I wasn't chosen. Not at first. Then one day my huMan came for me. I was so excited! He talked to me and rubbed my head and gave some colored pieces of paper to the human who lived in the house where I was chained and we were off to my new life.

Of course I wanted to please my huMan and make him proud of me so he would love me and keep me with him always. So when we went to my new job, I wanted to do my very best. My job was to play rough with the other dogs there in a kind of competition. I wasn't much of a fighter so it took me a while to learn what it was all about.

At first I thought it was a fun game. I was young and mixing it up with other dogs is what we like to do. These dogs were not having fun. They were serious about wanting to hurt me. Even when I wasn't in the thick of it, I could see what was going on with other dogs. Some of them hit the ground and never got up. It didn't take long for me to figure out that my new job was to stay alive.

Many were the nights I went home with my huMan bleeding and scarred. I licked my own wounds and a few days later we'd be back at the same place doing the same thing. One day he left me there and went away. I was only doing this for him and he wasn't even there. I waited and watched for him to come back. I stopped watching the games and went to the gate. I guess my crying annoyed the other humans there because one of them opened the gate and I took off.

I walked and ran for a long time, sleeping in the wild and foraging for food wherever I could find it. Eventually I ended up in a little village where gentle dogs wandered cobblestone streets. I didn't trust any of them. If they tried to get too close to me I barked and lunged at them until they ran away. I decided this time I would dictate the terms of the game.

As I wandered the streets I steered clear of danger. Because of my history, my senses to pain and suffering were heightened. I picked up on a heavy aura of both coming under the door of a little house I was walking past. I stopped. Sat. She opened the door. I continued to sit. The pain from her washed over me like hot lava. I couldn't move. If I did, her pain would have been worse... maybe fatal.

In spite of her pain, she was friendly. I let her touch me. We walked together to a place where she got food I really like. I don't know how she knew I'd like that kind especially. The same way I knew she was in pain, I guess. The food was the beginning of a good friendship. Then she stepped out of bounds.

One day she insisted I come into her house. She put one of those things on my neck that I hate and attached another thing to it like the chain used to be. While this thing wasn't a chain, I still couldn't get away. Not without hurting her, which I could never do. So I let her know I didn't want to be in her house and she got the message.

I went to her every day. She was my source of food and my new job. Taking care of her, feeling her pain get weaker and weaker, sharing walks with her and protecting her outside her front door...these were all the things I woke up for every morning. Maybe one of the reasons I was so happy was that I chose her. I remember how it felt never to be chosen. She didn't have to add that to her pain. I think she got better because I chose her.

I'm in a position to know that now. You see, one day before she woke up, I went on patrol around the neighborhood. I was checking out an area where some guys had been putting bricks together with muddy stuff in between them. Whatever they were making was getting bigger every day. Dogs like to hang around there and see what's going on. I liked to check those dogs out because they were close to her house. I'd had to kick some butt there a couple of times.

I was surprised when I arrived to see a thick paper with food on it. Really nice food. Raw. I hadn't had breakfast yet and none of the other dogs had come out, so I waded right in. I was half-way through it before I noticed that it didn't taste like any raw food I'd had in the past. I mean, I've eaten rotten and this wasn't rotten. It just tasted strange.

I got really thirsty and there was no water around. I guess the thirst caused the inside of my mouth to foam up, which was really unpleasant for as long as I noticed it. The dizziness distracted me and then the pain in my muscles as they stiffened up really got my attention. I had to lay down and rest until all this went away because she needed me. And I just couldn't make even the short walk to her house... rest... darkness.

To Live and Die in Peace

During the dry season along the north shore of Lake Chapala, strenuous activity is best enjoyed in the early morning or late evening. It was late evening in May 2012 when Daisy and her black Lab housemate started up the mountain with their huMan. It was a walk the three of them enjoyed often. It was to be their last. In a random act of violence almost unheard of in this idyllic community, the Lab was shot dead. Daisy and her huMan escaped to their home.

Soon thereafter, the family decided to return to their European homeland. They used e-mails to friends as well as social networking to sell their belongings and find a home for their Weimaraner. At age 12, they worried that Daisy would be hard to place. Not so.

Understanding the family's situation, Tim and Arlene Schubert stepped up immediately to bring Daisy into their home where she could run and play with Addie and Margo who were her own size.

The first few days were difficult for Daisy. Her former owner came every day for the first three or four days. He walked with Tim, Daisy, Addie, and Margo up the mountain and back. On two occasions, he even took Daisy home to spend the night and then brought her back for the walk up the mountain with her new housemates.

Daisy had always been an outdoor dog. Her bed went on the veranda of the Schubert home, giving her the safety of being inside and the comfort of the outdoors. Eventually, her bed went into Tim and Arlene's bedroom. The first night, Daisy just stood in the doorway and blinked her eyes, not knowing what to do with that arrangement.

It wasn't long before Daisy was sleeping in Tim and Arlene's room and hiking up the mountain every day like she was five years old instead of 12. Addie and Margo took her in and made her one of the pack. Margo, the black Standard Poodle, taught Daisy that the sofas in the house were perfect for daytime naps. The brindle mixed-breed Addie showed her how to engage humans in play.

For almost nine months, Daisy's life was happy and peaceful again.

My life was good and very good.

In late February 2013, Daisy stopped eating. She was lethargic. She had blood in her stool and was drinking as if to quench a constant thirst. The immediate diagnosis was rat poisoning. Following an injection to reverse the effects of the poison, the vet expected to see her blood coagulating. It did not. The final diagnosis was auto-immune disease, which caused her body to recognize her own blood as foreign. A transfusion did not help.

After surviving a traumatic brush with violence, Daisy was gone on the fifth day of her illness. "Those nine months with her were precious," Arlene said. And, indeed, they may have been for Daisy as well. She had the opportunity to cross the Rainbow Bridge from a place of peace and serenity, much like the one she had enjoyed for most of her life.

Saying Goodbye is Never Easy

As a very young girl growing up surrounded by nature in Newfoundland, Canada, she dreamed of becoming an artist. She was always able to see the beauty in people, objects and places. This would be one of her saving graces over her lifetime and a quality for which she was recognized and loved.

Shirley was a natural beauty herself. In fact, as a young woman she was runner-up to Miss Tomato Crop in the Montreal area. She wanted more… mainly to express herself artistically. So she enrolled in Ottawa Technical High School, which was an all-boys school except for the art program. Her looks were greatly appreciated by her classmates who enthusiastically vied for her attentions. Still, she kept focused.

She married a military man and they had three sons. Her husband died far too young and she raised those three hooligans alone. They became responsible, loving men who adored their mother.

To give her boys everything she could, Shirley had to take jobs that diverted her from her artistic pursuits. Many times those jobs required her to be creative and innovative in order to help her see the positive side of her circumstances. She never lost her smile and optimistic outlook. Everything was possible for her and her family.

Wanting to escape the brutality of Ottawa winters, Shirley became a "snowbird" visiting warmer, sunnier climates… Cuba, Malta… and finally she found the perfect spot… Mexico.

Moving to Lake Chapala in 1998 allowed her to resume her first passions… painting and pastels. Shirley became well known in the artists' community at Lakeside. Aging took its toll and she began to have back problems, which curtailed her career as an artist.

Her boys were grown, two living in Canada, one at Lakeside. Shirley needed a new passion. She had never had a dog. One day in 2000, while shopping at the Libertad Market in Guadalajara, she spied a dirty little creature whose hair was so matted she described it as looking like it had the dreadlocks of a Rastafarian. It clearly needed some tender, loving care.

Shirley and Perita — hearts of gold.

She took that little thing home, cleaned it up and loved it. It turned out to be a PLT (Poodle-Like-Thing) with white fluffy curls and a loving personality … much like Shirley's. Both had hearts of gold and really were soul mates. Shirley called her new best friend Perita.

They had a lovely life together until a day in 2002, when Shirley came home and Perita was gone. Two nights later she received a phone call… a man said he had "found" her dog and would return it to her for $100 dollars. Shirley agreed to meet him the next day. He had his young daughter with him. She was holding Perita and crying… "Please, please don't take my puppy," she pleaded. Typical of Shirley's caring nature, she let the little girl keep "her" dog… and gave them 500 pesos.

Living in Ajijic, Shirley observed many stray dogs that she called "street-walkers." Two in particular caught her attention … another little white PLT whom she took in and called Brinca… and a little black PLT waif that she named Chinita.

And there was Daisy. She had been hanging around the front

door of the house. Shirley took her in, cleaned her up and loved her. It turned out Daisy had a very serious form of epilepsy. Shirley got her on medication and found a friend who dearly wanted to look after Daisy until she crossed over the Rainbow Bridge... which was only a few weeks later.

Brinca was the boss of the house... a very strong personality and full of life. She was a mix of no-nonsense and cuteness. No one pushed her around. She was affectionate and loved to cuddle. She peed like a male dog, lifting her leg... perhaps to demonstrate her dominance. She didn't just walk... she skipped. Every few steps her left back leg would pull up, like a hippity-hop step.

Chinita & Shirley: Trekkers.   Brinca the Boss.

Chinita was sweet natured and, like Shirley, loved to love everyone. They had a unique and special bond. She licked Shirley's ankles... all the time. It was her way of showing her devotion. Shirley said that soft pink tongue was the best moisturizer she ever had!

They all slept together, cuddling and keeping each other warm. One of their favorite activities was watching snuggled up together in the easy chair... watching Star Trek. When they were together The Force was with them.

Everyone was aging. In 2011, Chinita's health began to fail. She could no longer control her bodily functions. She moved very slowly.

Shirley's son, Mike, would come to visit. When he sat on the couch Chinita would sit in front of him, looking at him longingly. He would not let her on the couch in case she had an accident. He did not fully understand her haunting look at him. When it was time for her to cross over the Rainbow Bridge, Mike spared his Mom the sadness of the decision. He took Chinita to Dr. Pepe. He held her in his arms. As Dr. Pepe gave her the injection, she turned her head, looked at Mike and thanked him with her eyes. Then, he knew.

Brinca didn't understand where Chinita had gone. She was lonely and would spend hours lying by the front door waiting for her pal who never returned.

In 2012, Shirley had a serious stroke and was bedridden. Brinca was no longer able to jump up onto the bed. The caregivers would lift her up. She would rub her nose on the covers to express how happy she was to be with her Shirley … then settle in pressed against her huMom.

Shirley never recovered from her stroke and died in May of 2012.

That day Brinca collapsed on the floor, overcome with grief. She wouldn't eat. She was listless. She wandered around aimlessly and then just flopped down with a sigh. Again she would lie by the front door… waiting.

Mike got her a new bed… well several beds… one for each room. She would curl up, and hang her head over the edge, blissful. Mike took her out and gave her lots of affection. She got back into life. She was skipping again.

In 2013, Mike came home one day to find Brinca half in and half out of a bed. One of her front paws was shaking. She did not look well. She got up and came towards him, walking like a drunken sailor, bumping into things and breathing heavily. He picked her up and took her to Dr. Pepe. She had had a stroke and her heart was enlarged.

They tried medication and injections. Neither seemed to help. Brinca mostly stayed in bed. Mike came back from doing errands and couldn't find Brinca. He called her name and heard a faint "arf" from the back yard. Brinca was lying under the avocado tree in the sun, with a smile on her face.

Mike knew she was telling him it was her time. He took her to Dr Pepe. He could not hold her. He could not watch. He left the room.

Going home, he thought, "I'm so glad I don't have to tell my Mom."

Winston Churchill

I am a Pug. No one has ever described me as handsome. Like the huMan I'm named for, I am more distinguished. Partially, this is due to the general shape and lack of contours to my face. Neither of us suffers fools gladly and, as such, I have no use for the creatures in our house known as cats. My legs are short, which only restricts me from a few activities. Quite frankly, the humans in my house compensate for my diminutive stature rather well.

My breathing patterns are unique… and to some unsophisticated and uneducated folk they may be considered disagreeable. If they find me offensive, I'm happy to return the favor.

My eyes and ears do not function as well as they used to. Again, care of these minor irritants is the purview of my people. They did try to have some small growths removed from my facial area in the hope that this would improve my looks… a somewhat unsuccessful operation, I must say. I remain, uniquely charming… and dignified.

I enjoy strolling on the promenade with my humans. I have developed a loyal following in the general area of the malecon and along the lakeshore. People seem to enjoy my presence and the opportunity to touch me and speak to me. They all treat me with the respect I am due.

I have a place of honor to lay my head at night. It's used by me and only me and affords me a very restful sleep and sweet dreams. When I awake each day, my huMan lifts me onto the bed. I roll on my back and he scratches my stomach. Rather an undignified pose, I agree. Yet in the privacy of one's bedroom, certain indiscretions may be tolerated.

The parallels to my namesake are uncanny. To paraphrase him, "Our tastes are simple: we are easily satisfied with the best." My humans always ensured that was true for my short and fulfilled life with them.

At age 90, he left this world… thus, not surprisingly, that was my age in dog years when I crossed the Rainbow Bridge.

A grand old man.

Who Rescued Who 2?

Loyal Companions

Every once in a while
A dog enters your life
And changes everything.

Author unknown

First Lord of the Admiralty... and Captain of Their Hearts

In 1997, it was New York City's loss and Ajijic's gain when Larry and Thetis Reeves moved south.

From the hustle and bustle of one of the world's busiest cities to a tranquil village Lakeside was quite a move. They found it easy to settle into their new community... Thetis began writing Pet columns for the local English language monthlies. Larry worked to modernize the Library at the Lake Chapala Society (LCS). They were living comfortably with their two cats and all was right in their world.

Thetis would market dogs for the animal shelter... telling their stories in order to get them adopted to forever homes. One unlikely charmer caught her eye. He was a nine-year-old Pug. He would be difficult to get adopted. Not because he was a Pug... because he was so old.

She wrote his story and circulated his photo to everyone she knew. It always got the same reaction, "He looks like Winston Churchill," and no offers of a home.

As there were no takers for him, Thetis thought she and Larry could take him on. Because of his distinguished appearance, they had to name him Winston Churchill. The cats' reaction was not quite as positive. One of them moved to the 2nd floor of the house and never came down again. The other got used to Winston over time.

Winston adapted well. He had no regard for the cats. He had some physical challenges with his eyes and ears, mainly due to his age. His stature (very short legs) prevented him from jumping onto their bed to sleep... well, jumping anywhere actually. Sometimes they would lift him onto the bed and sometimes he slept on a beautiful brocade pillow in a puffy dog bed. And they could always hear him coming with that characteristic Pug-ish snort and sniffle way of breathing.

He was a handsome old guy who loved to socialize. He was popular with everyone. Mexicans would giggle and point to him, calling him "Gordo" because of his size.

After four years, Winston crossed over the Rainbow Bridge suddenly and tragically. He and Larry were out doing errands one day and he leapt out of the car a little too quickly. He was hit by another car and died instantly.

Larry and Thetis were overwhelmed with grief. As they buried their beloved Winston in the garden, they vowed never to have another dog.

Nearly a year later, their resolve was tested… mightily. They could not imagine having another dog and certainly not a high maintenance puppy. They were not prepared for all the time and energy that would take. A friend told them of a poor dog who desperately needed a home… "He looks a little like a Pug," she said. Thetis tried to be firm when she said "No." The people who were fostering the poor waif already had four dogs and were returning north of the border. They invited Thetis and Larry to meet the dog and begged them to reconsider. Thetis kept repeating to herself, 'No, no, no." Then Larry said, quietly, "Well he is awfully cute."

That sealed the dog's fate. He had maneuvered his way into the household and their hearts… well, Thetis and Larry's hearts. He became known as Sonny. The cats still look at him with disdain.

Not a Pug

Pug, Pug, Pug, Pug, Pug… what's with the obsession with Pugs? I'm not a Pug. And yet the reason I'm where I am is because I look a little like a Pug. I have a malocclusion of the mouth… all that means is I should have wires on my teeth. Apparently that's what makes me resemble the famous Pug. Quite frankly, I can live with the situation.

I'm actually of mixed heritage, in that attractive Mexican street dog kind of way. At my size and weight, I'm small enough to get away with being a lap dog, and big enough not to be… if I want. I mean if there's an open lap and I like you… I'm there!

Larry and Thetis didn't really want a dog… and if they did, they thought they wanted a Pug… and guess what… they picked me! I thought I'd won the lottery. That was short-lived. On the way home, they stopped and we all got out of the car. I was on a table; I got poked with a tiny sharp stick and… boom! I was down for the count. Out cold. Woke up after a nice sleep, stood up and… whoa, wait a minute… what's that pain in my… uh, rear-end area. Just let me sit down… oh no, not a good idea… more pain. I just took it easy for a few days… not a lot of sitting.

I had some serious exploring to do. There are so many spots to run and sniff and hide. This is a nice place… inside and out. Lots of house and lots of garden. There're these two cats that live here too. I try to play with them… you know, I get in my downward dog pose and I bob and weave and look at them and they… well, they just look down their noses at me, flick their tales and sashay away. I heard Thetis call them "prima donnas." I'm not sure if that's a good thing or not. One of them is a real snob. She stays upstairs and takes naps on a fancy pillow that belonged to… guess what? A Pug!

Now, the one thing those cats do that I like is, we all sleep on the bed together! I know! Is that a great idea or what? I've got a lot of energy so I run around a bunch. When I see Thetis and Larry get into the bed… and then those cats… I know it's my turn. I take one last dash around the house and then I leap from the door and land on the bed! Cool, huh? Everybody laughs… except, of course, the cats.

In the morning, Larry and I get up first because we're guys and we have stuff to do. He makes coffee and I supervise. He sits down on his chair in the office and I jump on his lap. That way I can go back to sleep while he's looking at this box thingy. Sometimes he scratches my ears… I just love that.

Guy stuff.

Me, Larry and Thetis go in the car a lot… nah-nah cats… they can't go. I get pretty excited when I know it's time for a car ride. I play a game with Larry… catch me buddy… he holds a ropey thing, he calls me and chases me a bit, I run around 'til I'm tired and then I flop down in front of him. He attaches the ropey thing to my collar and off we go.

I know Thetis and Larry like me even though I'm not… say it with me now…a Pug! And I really, really, really like them.

Muneca Incarnate

Kateri Brown's sweet little white dog, Muneca, was the great love of her life.

Muneca had belonged to a Mexican family and seemed always to be living on the streets. In 2004, Kateri was new and a little lost herself in Puerto Vallarta when Muneca adopted her. Already nine years old, Muneca and Kateri were together another eight years. She was old and wise and could always read Kateri's thoughts. When Muneca crossed the Rainbow Bridge, Kateri grieved for nine months.

Great things can happen when you look
like someone who was loved.

Then something amazing happened. A friend in Puerto Vallarta saw a little dog that looked just like Muneca on the SPCA Facebook page. Sending Kateri the link, she wrote, "Don't you think it's time for another Muneca in your life?"

Kateri looked through the nine photos of the dog, whose shelter name was Cody, and fell in love. She felt like Muneca had been reincarnated into this sweet little white angel that looked exactly like her. Kateri, who was in Oregon at the time, asked two friends to visit him at the shelter and check him out. They reported back that he was just like Muneca and even better...so mellow and relaxed..."like a noodle."

A voice inside Kateri's head kept saying, "No! No! Don't do this," while her heart-driven fingers were writing the e-mail to start the adoption process. Kateri drove to Puerto Vallarta three weeks later to pick up her new little buddy before heading home to Ajijic.

Kateri thinks Vinny Blanco Brown (he is no longer Cody) is what Muneca must have been like as a puppy. His looks, his temperament, his personality are all consistent with the adult Muneca who came into Kateri's life at age nine.

A Mama's Boy

I'm Vinny Blanco Brown and I'm from Puerto Vallarta. I lived on the streets there when I was a puppy. It's a happening place, so I didn't really mind. Plus, I used to get to go on these reeeeeeeeeeeeeeeally long sleep-overs where there were lots of other dogs to play with.

The second time I was at one of those long sleepovers, Kateri...that's her name, isn't it beautiful?...she's my huMom. Anyway, she came and picked me up. She was so sweet. I could tell right away that she loved me. It made me feel warm and tingly all over. The first thing we did was go on a long car ride and I lay right up against her the whole way.

Bright and early the morning after we got here, we went for a long walk beside this huuuuuuuuuuuge puddle of water. I hear Mom call it "the lake." We do that every single morning now. It's our routine. There's this giant wide sidewalk beside the lake where I run into so many friends to play with. Mom calls it "the malecon." As if that wasn't enough fun, guess what happened next?

Okay, I'll tell you. Mom's friend Mark has a tiny black and white spotted Chihuahua who's a little bit older than me. Her name is Vaca. Her Mark was traveling so Vaca got to be with us. She's kind of adopted me. To tell you the truth, I think she has a bit of a crush on me. I don't mean to sound vain or anything. Here's what makes me think that.

I'm about twice her size so I let her take the lead. I'd never want to play too rough or do anything to hurt her. She taught me this game and we play it a lot now. We "mouth" each other and make squeaky noises like we're two squeaky toys biting at each other. It's just we don't bite. You see what I mean? Wouldn't you think somebody who taught you a game like that had a crush on you?

That's my wired friend, Vaca. Isn't she a doll?

Vaca sleeps over with us pretty often. I'm not a morning dog. I'd be content to lollygag on my back for hours in the morning getting my belly rubbed, or just chilling out. Vaca, on the other hand, has four spring-loaded paws. She's up. She's running. She's getting everybody else up. Let's go! Rise 'n' shine! Little girl wears me out just thinking about her.

Lots of times Mom takes us both for a ride in the car. Vaca boings into the car and picks her place to sit. I just curl up wherever she isn't, as long as it's next to my Mom or on her lap. Vaca may be the princess… I know I'm my Mama's boy.

Constant Companions

"I've always been a dog person," says Evelyn Fleming. And she's had all sizes, shapes and breeds of them in her life. Born in Manitoba, Canada, she lived most of her life in Toronto and then the Ottawa area. When she retired in 1981, she built her dream cottage on a lovely lake in Halliburton. After a few years, the winters became a little too taxing. She moved to Prescott and lived on a golf course. She could pursue her passion for golfing whenever she wanted.

In 2008, her son, David, retired to Ajijic. He showed his Mom some photos of where he was going. That got her interested in joining him. Once he was settled, she and her Yorkie-Poo, Pepe, arrived for an extended visit. They landed late at night and didn't get to see much. When Evelyn awoke in the casita, she saw it was all glass on one side and she was looking at a swimming pool surrounded by lush gardens and poinsettia trees! There was color everywhere.

She joined David on the terrace for a scrumptious breakfast. He asked if she wanted to call her friends back in Canada to let them know she arrived safely. Everyone asked the same question, "How do you like Mexico?" and her responses varied from, "I'm in seventh heaven" to, "My first impression is, I love it" and, "I feel like I'm in paradise." Pepe also enjoyed all the new sights and sounds to investigate.

Evelyn did some serious house hunting and found a perfect spot for her and Pepe. They returned to Canada, got rid of most of their things and came back to their new life in Mexico.

After a couple of years, Pepe began to gain weight and her energy level dropped dramatically. Fearing it was more than natural ageing, Evelyn took her to the vet. Pepe was diagnosed with severe diabetes and soon crossed over the Rainbow Bridge.

They had been the closest of companions for 14 years and

Evelyn missed Pepe desperately. She knew she wanted another dog for company. So the search began. She was looking for something small.

The girls

Evelyn visited Anita's… nothing fit her criteria. She went to the animal shelter… only medium and large dogs there. She thought of a creative approach. She would go to a vet and tell him what she was looking for. If he heard of, or had the occasion to deliver a litter, she wanted him to let her know and she would take one. As she turned to leave the vet's office she saw a picture of the cutest little bundle of white fluff. The vet told her a woman had put up the sign that day. She was fostering the little darling and it needed a home. Her big dog did not appreciate its presence in his domain! The woman had to take the dog to bed with her to protect her during the night. Evelyn called the woman and was told she needed to be interviewed. They arranged a time for the next day.

Once Maya, the sweet natured little Poodle-Maltese mix, and Evelyn laid eyes on each other it was love at first sight. The interview ended up being a formality.

The two "girls" are now constant companions, watching and loving each other's every move.

YOLO... You Only Live Once

Hi, hi, hi, hi, hi... I'm Maya. I'm two years old in human years, so that's like 14 in dog years, right? I used to run the streets of Chapala and, that was literally a lot of work and not much fun. I'm white and fluffy so I get dirty pretty fast, and, Dude like that's so not good, ya know?

This awesome lady, she took me home and bathed me, right? And she was really nice. She had this big dog that was such a bully, right? And he would like get all in my face and keep me in a corner. So, like, I had to sleep with the woman in her bed so she could keep me safe from him, right?

I could not stay there... I mean, duh. So the lady found like another lady to take me home. Seriously, this new lady, called Evelyn, she and I bonded like right away. It was pretty intense.

Evelyn, she like has this epic little house and she, um, had this little red bed for me. Yeah, whatever! I use it to like nap in the day. She found out the first night that I was like sleeping with her, right? It's a good thing too. Seriously, I sleep by her feet and when she starts moving around I know she's got pain in her legs... ewww. So I lick them to make her feel better. Dude, sometimes it's really bad for her. I literally almost lick off her skin.

Evelyn is a very particular lady. We both always want to look our best... not blingy, just classy, right? Sometimes she'll say to me, "You kind of smell stinky, Maya." So then I go in the shower with her. After, she tells me I smell pretty. And like so does she... always.

Oh, snap! I have to tell you this really funny thing. Evelyn has this cool doll that plays music... something about a twinkling star... anyway, it's a pretty catchy little tune. When I hear it I get on my hind legs and I twirl. Evelyn laughs and sometimes she takes my front paws in her hands and we twirl together... cool, huh?

Now, Evelyn likes to talk... she's a really good storyteller and she has like lots of stories to tell. Seriously, Dude, in dog years, she's like over 600! Niiiiice, huh! I watch her when she talks and I move my mouth like hers. No sounds come out... so I'm like not really talking, right? Yet. When people come to visit, I sit with them and listen and move my mouth too.

Sometimes at night, we hear big sounds. Evelyn has to turn up the volume on the TV. I just sigh... I mean, what*ever*.

I go everywhere with Evelyn... to look after her. When she says my name I wag my tail, because she's like really special, right? Sometimes I like see bugs (ewwwww) or scorpions (seriously ewwwww) and I show Evelyn where they are. She whacks them with like a shoe and they're goners, Dude.

Oopsie, I almost forgot to tell you what a good cook she is. Like, literally, she makes me the best stuff to eat. She like so knows how much I enjoy chicken and bacon, right? She makes that a lot. And she mixes in that kibble stuff. I have to eat it. Later.

You know, Dude, YOLO (you only live once) so, I'm like glad I'm doing it with Evelyn, right? She is awwwwwwwwwwwwwwwwesome, Dude.

Do I wanna dance? Oh yeah!

A Chilango in Chapala

Marti Heismann took a circuitous route from Hawaii to Chapala, via Florida and Ixtlahuacan de los Membrillos, a village a few miles north of Lake Chapala. She arrived in 2010 and settled on Zaragoza Prolongacio in what she refers to as "the country." She loved her Mexican neighbors, their delightful children, and the buzzing and humming of cottage businesses along her street, which included a carpinteria, or woodworking shop, at the end.

As part of the ebb and flow of life in her neighborhood, Marti often saw a parade of women and children being led down the street by a very small gray terrier mixed breed dog. Clearly he did not know he was small. He strutted like a high school drum major as he led his entourage to the abarrotero. Once at the little grocery store, he received a treat.

In time, Marti joined the group down the lane, turning left toward the store. She was quite taken by this little dog who backed down Dalmatians and Rottweilers as he strutted his stuff through what appeared to be his turf. Her Mexican neighbors told her that dogs see one another's energy field, not physical size, and that is what dictates dominance.

Marti learned that the dog was called Chilango. Chilango is a slang term for a resident of Mexico City. The little guy seemed to live in and around the carpinteria, which was closed on weekends. Chilango sometimes came to Marti's house on weekends for food. One time when he was at her house, she could see he was very sick. Someone came to get him and she didn't see him for a week.

Walking out the door, headed for the airport to pick up a friend from Hawaii, Marti got a call from Carlos, a Mexican neighbor. Chilango was there and very, very sick. Marti asked Carlos to take him to the vet and she would pay when she returned. Carlos later told her she had saved Chilango's life, so now she had to keep him.

Marti's macho Chapalino.

Together, Carlos and Marti went to the carpinteria to inquire into Chilango's story. They learned that he had arrived four or five years ago with a craftsman from Mexico City who did poor quality work. When he lost his job, he left Chilango behind.

Chilango is a Chapalino now. Since 2011, Marti has called him Nacho and he responds. Together they moved to a different Chapala neighborhood, close to Christiana Park where Nacho loves to walk.

Marti always had rescue dogs in Hawaii and on the U.S. mainland. Nacho has insinuated himself into her life and made her house a real home. Marti says, "I am always grateful for allowance into a dog's world."

Macho Nacho Man. Everybody Loves the Nacho Man

My name wasn't always Nacho. I guess you could say I had a life-changing experience a couple of years ago. Let me tell you about it.

I grew up in Mexico City, and like Mexico City, I'm huge. I moved here to the sticks with my companion guy back in about 2005 on the people calendar. That really means nothing to me. I'm just tryin' to make it easy for you. He found work at a local carpinteria. His job was to make stuff out of wood. My job was to protect my turf and make it safe for folks to find their way to their food.

I was good at my job. My companion, not so much. He was asked to leave. I stayed behind to keep doin' my job. When I got folks to their food, I always got food for myself there, too. I made friends real easy in the barrio. I was what you'd call a "guy's guy."

Things seemed to change in the barrio. For a while, the carpinteria where I stayed was closed. I had nothing to eat except what a nice gringa fed me when I went to her house. Since it was my job to take care of folks in my barrio, I didn't want to go around beggin' for food. Bad for my image. I got pretty sick. Almost died. When I got better, the gringa invited me to live with her.

Her name is Marti. Isn't that the most beautiful name you ever heard? My name used to be Chilango until Marti changed it to Nacho. Frankly, I don't care what she calls me, as long as she calls me. Marti talks to me a lot and I understand everything she says. I'm bilingual.

Marti and I moved from the old barrio to a house in Chapala. My old friend, Carlos, comes with some workers sometimes.

They bring power tools and trimmers and snappers and stuff. All that buzzing reminds me of the carpinteria and what used to be my home.

My home is with Marti now. I'm still pretty regimented from my time on my turf, so I've set up a routine here. She begins to prepare breakfast for me and I bring out all my little soft doll babies. I put them in lines facing up and let them know they're going to have breakfast, too. I know they aren't real, so it's okay if they don't actually eat.

After breakfast, I get the leash so Marti knows it's time to go to Christiana Park. I have so many fans there. I love it when I'm strutting through the park with Marti and one of the guys calls out, "Hey there, Macho Nacho!" That'd be me.

Time for breakfast, mis bebés.

Restoring Balance

R obyn had been in Ajijic for three years when 2007 brought tragedy into her life. Two very close friends died suddenly within three weeks of each other. With great compassion for Robyn in her grief, a neighbor gave her a three-year-old dog named Camilla. It was such a healing experience for Robyn to bond with Camilla. The two of them were devoted to each other for the next three years. Until Camilla got very sick with something undiagnosable and crossed the Rainbow Bridge from Robyn's arms.

Grief returned. Robyn was having difficulty sleeping, which made her feel even worse. The house felt lopsided… like it was tipping. With Camilla gone, there was no counterbalance on the bed. Or in the house.

About two weeks later, a foster mom walked into Robyn's gallery with a honey-colored PLT (Poodle-Like-Thing). As Robyn made a fuss over the dog, she learned her name was Miel. She went on to tell how Miel was the only survivor of an old home remedy gone tragically bad.

Miel, her mother, and all of her siblings had sarcoptic mange. They were covered in motor oil in order to cure it. Miel was the only survivor of the treatment and she was in a coma when she was rescued.

When she finally awoke from her coma, the vet began treating her mange with a series of injections. She was one shot short of completion when Robyn met her. Robyn asked to adopt the little fluff ball and by week's end, Robyn and Miel were a family.

Miel, Mieli, or Mielicita, as Robyn sometimes calls her, is full of fun and love and cuddles. Robyn takes her everywhere, from local restaurants to the beach. She's very sociable with other dogs and she loves people. She jumps and plays and runs in and out of her neighbors' houses, truly at home on her little privada.

We are family.

At the end of the day Miel goes to sleep in her own bed. Later she jumps on Robyn's bed and makes a cave out of the pillows and covers. Then she stretches out on her back and falls asleep as Robyn sings to her.

The house and the bed are back in balance. And so is Robyn's life.

Honey Bunch

Habla usted español? Do you speak Spanish? My name is Miel. It means "honey" in Spanish. When I was very small, folks called me Mieli. Robyn still calls me Mielicita sometimes. It makes me sound even sweeter than I am. And I'm very sweet. Everybody says so.

My street is short and very private because there is only one-way in and out. Robyn and I live near the end and I know all our neighbors. I love to visit one of them across the street and investigate alla the stuff in the back yard. They have lizards and birds and I love to watch them. Sometimes when I go there the papacito, who Robyn calls the patriarch of the family, is sitting on his bench in the yard. When he is, I jump right up and curl in beside him. Then we watch everything together.

I go everywhere with Robyn. Por que? Know why? Because I'm so good. I learned very soon after I came to live with her that if I wanted to go places, I had to behave like a lady. When we go where humans eat… they sit in chairs and eat off of flat surfaces in front of them… I sit in a chair too. When I'm in my chair, I'm dignified. I just watch. I never beg for any food.

Robyn and I go walking along the lakeshore. I love it! Sometimes, if something catches my eye, I run into the water to see what it is… a toy? a stick? a morsel of something tasty? A girl never knows for sure unless she investigates. In case you missed it, I'm an investigator. When we go to the ocean, I stay on the sandy beach. Ocean water? Yuk! Pfitt! Did you ever taste that stuff?

At home I only bark to let Robyn know someone is at our door or close by the outside of our house. Robyn seems to like it when I do that. I love to please Robyn because I love her so much. Sometimes she does things I don't like. I don't like to get my coat brushed. I go under the bed and into the corner and just sit until her urge to brush me passes.

I'm very happy almost all of the time. Every once in a while... not very often at all...Robyn wants me to do something I don't want to do. I sulk. She's unimpressed. We work it out...her way...because she's the Mamacita.

Habla usted español?

I'm not a morning person. I'm up early in the afternoon, having a nice comida, planning my adventures for the day. Then I'm still having fun and playing until after dark. Robyn's that way, too. I usually go to bed before she does. When I hear her come into her big bed, I'm right there beside her. I fluff up my own space and stretch out on my back. The last thing I hear at the end of the day is her sweet voice singing to me.

I love her so much.

Two-fer

athie and Gregg Byers are "snowbirds" who spend six months of the year Lakeside and six months in the United States on another lake. During the time they spend in Mexico, they immerse themselves in the community. For example, a teacher by passion, Kathie coaches friends and neighbors in Spanish. And since 2010, they have changed the lives of five dogs and one cat.

The rescue of 2013 was different. Gregg was on his way to his weekly coffee group to solve the problems of the world… or at least those of his buddies at the table. As he was leaving, he saw a man throw two objects from a bag into the arroyo, a dry riverbed, near their house. He shouted, the man looked at him and ran off. Gregg went closer and looked down. He thought he saw two little puppies lying in the dry channel. They might have been moving, Gregg wasn't sure. He called out to Kathie. As she came running, he jumped down to the quivering little objects. He tried to pick one up. Both skittered away, as if they were joined together.

A neighbor came to their aid. Between them, they were able to pick up the white one and hand it to Kathie. The black one was more of a challenge. It scampered away every time someone got close. They were afraid it would run out onto the road and get hit by a car. A security guard joined the rescue effort. Finally the little black fur ball was captured.

Gregg and Kathie made a bed from a soft pillow and tried to feed the two tiny pups some water. They just lay together, touching, and barely moving, for almost 24 hours. They looked like yin and yang. Kathie called them Blanquito (little white one) and Negrita (little black one).

Kathie and Gregg were returning to their home in the US in a few weeks. They began to look for someone to take the puppies. Lucky Dogs Shelter was over-full. All of their friends already had dogs. The word went out to friends of friends… no takers.

These were a special pair. They could not… and would not…be separated. There just had to be a special home for both of them. Kathie's heart was breaking. She briefly considered having them put to sleep so they could be together for eternity.

Cannot be separated.

At last, a friend told a Mexican family in San Antonio about the dogs. The father came to look at the perritos and offered to take one. Kathie and Gregg were firm… it was both or none. They offered to have the dogs neutered, spayed and groomed. Another neighbor offered to provide beds and food. The man had to talk with his family.

He returned several days later. "Si," he said, his family would take care of the dogs… and he promised, they would always keep them together.

Before Kathie and Gregg left for the US, the entire family came to visit… with the dogs. There were tears of joy in Kathie's eyes as she said good-bye to the very special duo.

Together... Forever

"Take care of each other... and always stay together." Those were the last, desperate words we heard from our mother. Well, actually she said them in Spanish... we're using English so you can comprende; I mean understand, our story.

A horrible man shoved me... I'm the cute, black little girl... and my brother into a smelly old bag. We were rolling around in it, bumping into each other. It was hot and we couldn't breathe very well. My brother... the handsome little white one... started to whimper. "I'm here," I told him, "I'll take care of you."

Suddenly we were flying through the air and we slammed into the ground where it was rocky and hard and dusty. Everything hurt. I told my brother to lay still right next to me. And when we felt better we'd figure out what to do.

There was a lot of shouting and it seemed like humans were everywhere. We got separated and a lady took my brother away. I was mad. Every time someone came close to me I snapped and growled. I was running around and around the human who was holding my brother. I was barking and barking. "Put him down," I was saying. "He's my brother and I must take care of him."

A human grabbed me... I was sore and tired. I just gave up. The person put me on something soft, right beside my brother. We both sighed. The humans were gently putting water on our lips. It felt good. We both fell asleep.

When I woke up, my brother was gone. I was whining, "Oh no, oh no. Where is he?" I'd promised our mother I would take care of him. I lay very still and whimpered.

I heard a familiar bark and looked up. It sounded like my brother. It sure didn't look like him. His hair was very short. I sniffed him all over. It didn't smell like my brother... well not the

way he used to smell. This stranger lay down beside me...
aahhhhh, he felt like my brother. He was back.

Then it was my turn to go away and I knew he would be frightened so I told him it would be OK. I'd be back soon. And I was.
Now I looked and smelled fabulous too.

A man came to look at us and he spoke to us in Spanish... he
said he had a family. In his family is a little girl who needs a dog
to stay with her and take care of her. And the rest of the family
wanted a dog to play with. I tried to tell him, we would be perfect together. He went away.

Muchisimas gracias

The humans we lived with took us for walks. My brother
stayed right beside me when we walked. We slept together on
that soft thing. And we had food to eat and lots of water. We're
going to be together forever, "Just like our mother wanted," I
thought.

One day I heard, "Buenos dias," and the Mexican man was
back. He was talking to us in Spanish and telling us we were going to live at his house. My brother and I started jumping with
joy and wagging our tails and we went home with him. I play

with all the kids and the cousins. My brother sits quietly with the man's daughter. She pats him and talks to him. They stay close together like he and I used to. Everyone speaks Spanish here… we understand everything.

We miss our mother sometimes. I think she knows we're happy and together. To those very kind people who saved us we want to say, "Muchissimas gracias"… thank you sooooooooooooooooooooooo much.

The Lily Dog

When Jack and Kate Jerrett moved to Lakeside from Nova Scotia in 2011, the last thing on their minds was getting a dog. Their Cocker Spaniel had died three decades before. They enjoyed travel. "Dog" wasn't even in their vocabulary. Nope. Just didn't come up.

And then Kate read Who Rescued Who: Tales of Street Dogs and the People Who Love Them. Of course she had seen the street dogs. "You can't help but see them," she says. The book gave them voices, made their experiences real, and opened her heart.

She and Jack discussed it … talked about their friends who had a dog named Lily. Jack loved Lily. "If we can get a Lily dog," was his concession. Coincidentally, a very short time later her friend Barbara called to say, "Your dog has come into my garden!" The gardener shut the gate, and the dog jumped eight feet up the wall trying to get over it and out of the property. She bit Barbara as she reached for the dog. And as part terrier, she was a very fast runner.

Kate arrived and was finally able to approach the pathetic looking, nearly bald, pink-skinned critter. In addition to her obvious maladies, she was in heat. Kate gathered her up and took her to the vet, and then home.

"Okay, she can stay a week," Jack conceded. The "week" turned into forever. She doesn't leave his side, following him everywhere. As her fur grew back and her skin healed, she was called Little Orphan Annie.

Annie doesn't leave the house now, except to go for walks or chase Kate and Jack. Once she got through the fence and followed the car to the gate of their community where the maid found her. Another time she followed Jack to the house up the hill from theirs.

When Jack and Annie walk together, Annie is, of course, on a leash. As they make their rounds through the neighborhood, she has come to know the houses where other dogs live. She whines and cries as she passes them. Annie doesn't like other dogs.

I tell Kate everything for Jack.

Says Jack, "She simplifies my life. I don't have to tell Kate where I'm going. I tell Annie I'm going to the store and I'll be back in about 15 minutes." The best part about having Annie in their lives is her enthusiasm when they walk through the front door. Says Jack, "Who can look at you with the devotion in their eyes that a dog does. Talk about unconditional love, that's it."

Little Orphan Annie

Pssst, hi. I'm over here. I don't mean to appear rude. It's just that I'm a shy girl. I had a rough start on the streets. It makes me stay away from other dogs. I don't like them. Actually, I'm afraid of them. I was attacked by some dogs a while ago and it was so traumatic I can't even discuss it. A while later, I had a litter of puppies. I don't know what happened to them.

So one day I was walking along minding my own business and keeping a low profile when a bunch of male dogs came after me again. I was so scared. I ran through the grass and the next think I knew, a gate slammed shut behind me. I didn't know where the dogs were. I had to get out of there. A woman tried to stop me and I bit her. Finally, I got myself into a corner where I thought I'd be safe...for a little while.

While I was hiding out, I saw a lady come toward me with her hand out. She came slowly. Spoke softly. Maybe she'd get me out of here. I let her pick me up. She got me out all right, and into a bathtub and rubbed some smelly stuff on my body and did some poking and prodding. Humans are weird with all the stuff they say makes us dogs feel better. Okay, maybe I did feel better. Later.

Next she took me to a house and I got to go inside. That never happened before in my whole life. I don't know how long that was in years... human or dog years. Anyway, she took me to Jack. I love Jack! He calls her Kate.

I started sleeping in their house right away. I have my own bed in the room where they sleep. Jack wakes up really early in the morning and I wag my tail to let him know how happy I am to see him...I wag all the way from my tail to my shoulders. Before Jack and I leave the bedroom, I go to Kate's side of the bed and scratch on the bed covers. (I don't have bed covers. Jack and Kate don't have fur.) Sometimes Kate's hand will flop out and hang beside the bed, so I kiss it and kiss it and kiss it.

Pssst! I'm over here.

Then Jack and I go outside. He likes for me to walk him, so I do. When we come back and Kate's up, we play our favorite game. Jack will say, "Go find Kate," and I take off running around the house like I'm looking for her, sliding on the marble floor, bumping off the walls until I get to her. Then Kate says, "Go find Jack," and I do the same thing all over again in the other direction. It's good exercise for me and the best part is it makes them both laugh and laugh.

Sometimes Jack and Kate leave the house without me. I never do understand exactly why they do that. I'm a good dog. When I go in the car I sit on the front passenger seat. If Kate and Jack are both in the car, I sit on Kate's lap. Sometimes we go to restaurants together. I just lay down beside their feet under the table. I'm a very good dog in restaurants.

So I don't understand why I can't always go with them. I let them know I don't understand and I'm not happy about it. I sit under the table in the entrance of our house and look mournful. I cock my head. I look pathetic. Sometimes it works. Kate will go to the drawer where my leash is and I jump so high I can touch her shoulders!

I have stopped barking at the phone when it rings because I see that's something that Kate and Jack treat in a friendly way. I hate the noise the gate makes because I know Jack and Kate are leaving and if I can hear it, that means I'm not with them.

Some noises that seem to bother other dogs around here don't bother me at all. I don't even hear the fireworks, and thunder is just another sound in the air. The sound that does really get my attention is the family car pulling up to our door. That means Jack or Kate or both of them are home. I just sit at the door and wait for them. I don't make a sound. They are my whole world. When they walk through that door, my life is complete.

A Very Lucky Dog

She came from *New* Mexico to *Real* Mexico in 2010, looking for the quality of life and awesome weather that is found here in Lakeside.

Cameron Peters has always loved dogs...especially rescue dogs. Accompanying her on the move from Santa Fe to San Antonio Tlayacapan were two adopted dogs from Santa Fe... Xochi (SOshee), a 12-year-old mostly Border Collie, whose name means "flower" in Nahual; and Amore, a 10-year-old Australian Shepherd.

Cameron's volunteer activities have always included working with shelters. She became involved with Lakeside Friends of the Animals Foundation and sits on their board.

One day Cameron met a woman on the street who told her about a spay and neuter clinic for cats and dogs. The first one had been held in November of 2011. The surgeries are a free service for pets of Mexicans of limited means. The program was called Operación Amor. Cameron became a volunteer for the second clinic held in Santa Cruz in March of 2012. From then until July of 2013, five more clinics have been held, with Cameron as the Coordinator of Volunteers.

No one really wanted another dog in the family. Xochi and Amore had settled into a comfortable routine. Cameron's philosophy had always been "two hands, two dogs." And the informal rules in their compound allowed only two dogs per household.

That all changed on a fateful day in January 2013. It was Cameron's first day as a volunteer at Lucky Dog Rescue and Adoption Center.

While getting to know the dogs, Cameron was struck by one

in particular named Sheba. An attractive Husky-Shepherd mix, she sat very straight and made eye contact immediately. In fact, that eye contact went directly to Cameron's heart.

For two months she walked, fed and played with Sheba, bonding more and more every week… and falling more and more in love with the black haired beauty with six toes on each of her back feet.

Cameron and her girls love to hang out.

Then one day, Cameron arrived and Sheba was not there. She had been adopted. Cameron was surprised at how devastated she felt; like she had lost a dear friend. She worried about Sheba, thought of her every day, and hoped she had found the loving family she deserved.

The following week Sheba was back! Things had not worked out in the new home. That day, when Cameron went home, Sheba went with her.

Third Time Lucky

My name is Sheba. I'm black and beautiful, with bright white markings. Humans say I'm a mix of a Husky and a Shepherd … hmmm … guess that's how I got six toes on each back foot. I'm proud of who I am. I always sit up straight and look everyone in the eye. I've lived through bad times and good times and survived. I've been rescued three times!

I remember living in a crate at Dr. Pepe Magaña's office. He's a really nice man and the people who work in his office are nice too. They fed me and kept me clean. While it wasn't much fun in that cage-y thing, I did feel safe and secure in it. Dr. Pepe says I'm about two years old. I'm not sure what that means except I really prefer to run around than to be cooped up.

I moved to a place with lotsa other dogs and fields and grass and sunshine and fresh air … wow, it felt like freedom. Almost. I mean I couldn't exactly run and jump around free all the time. I did have to spend time in a cage-y thing again. I like sleeping in it.

And there was this really fun lady who came to see me. She would feed me and pet me and we'd go for walks and she'd talk to me. I would run and sniff stuff and she would laugh and talk to me more. I really liked the sound of her voice. She seemed like a special friend.

One day another lady came and looked at me and took me home. She went to work every day and I was at home alone. I missed seeing people and other dogs. I was really, really lonely. I was mopey and didn't want to eat. The lady took me back to the place with the other dogs.

When my special friend came in, she ran to my cage and opened it. Well, I was so happy to see her that I jumped right on her and licked her face … almost right off!. She started laughing and crying and hugging me. She fed me and we went for a walk and she was talking to me very seriously … about going to live at her house. I barked to tell her "yes, yes, yes" I wanted to live with her.

We got in her car and went to her house. I sat up straight on the seat and watched everything. We were getting close to some water. Oh my gosh, her house is right beside a lot of water. And sand. And sticks. And grass. And dead fish. Oh wow, this is gonna be good, I thought.

We went into the house … uh-oh. There were two old dogs there. They seemed a bit scary to me. I just sat down real straight and looked them in the eye.

It took a few months and now we have a civilized and respectful tolerance for each other. I actually play with the one called Amore. I like to tease her and get her to chase after me. I'll hide and she always finds me. The other one is called Xochi and she doesn't play much. She mostly watches us fool around … and sleeps.

That Xochi seems to be the one in charge. She told me all about her rules for getting up in the mornings. She decides when we all get up. First she and Amore get cuddles in bed. I get out of my crate and I sit right beside the bed and wait. I start to get so excited for my turn, my tail is wagging and I'm licking my lips and it seems to take forever. When our huMom puts her feet on the floor it's my turn! I can get my cuddles. Not on the bed, though.

Our huMom does lotsa stuff with us. Every morning we go for a freedom walk up a mountain. There are so many smells and plants and places to explore. At night we go for a walk on the beach, mostly on our leashes. Sometimes we're free. I like to look for dead fish and roll on them. Xochi and Amore (and huMom) just look at me, kinda disgusted.

Some days we go to Free Spirit Playpark and do stuff with other dogs. That's pretty fun. I get to see some of my old friends there.

At night we take our positions while our huMom lays in her hammock and reads. We know exactly where to be, right where her hand can reach us for a quick scratch behind the ears … or a rub on the head.

When it's time to go to sleep, I find my squeaky toy and go into my crate. It's nice and private in there; just me and my toys and my blankie. Xochi and Amore sleep on the bed with hu-Mom.

I'm proud to be part of this family and I won't ever need to be rescued again.

We Are Family

Theresa and her rescued Cock-a-Poo, Sweet Pea, arrived Lakeside in 2002. As they settled into their new life, Theresa considered looking for a companion, for both of them. The time just never seemed right.

Almost a year later, Sweet Pea crossed the Rainbow Bridge. Theresa missed her terribly and would not even consider another dog.

One sunny Wednesday, while in the tianguis, she was passing Anita's booth and noticed two dogs. That got her thinking, maybe it's time.

The following Wednesday, there was only one dog at Anita's booth. The folks there happened to have a leash, so Theresa took the dog for a walk, just to see if they might get along. The dog was very well behaved and they stopped for a coffee. The dog jumped right onto Theresa's lap and snuggled in.

This was a match. Theresa wanted her to have a Mexican name. She decided something regal would be appropriate. As a student of history, Theresa remembered the name Carlota. She was an empress, the wife of Maximillian… and Bette Davis played her in a movie. Carlota was the perfect name.

Carlota is a happy, spirited Schnauzer, Terrier and several other things mix who always attracts attention. She is an exuberant, joyful and friendly soul. She knows no strangers. When she encounters new people she leans in for her pat… and smiles.

Carlota and Theresa were creating their new routines when Theresa found a human companion. She and Carlota moved into his house. While he had some definite ideas about a dog and its place, Carlota soon changed his mind.

They became a family and spent several years together. Sadly, the gentleman became incurably ill, was moved to a care facility and passed away.

Carlota was the best nurse and companion. She never demanded attention; she took herself outside when she needed to. She kept a close watch, only barking if someone came too close to the front door.

Just the two of us... looking good.

She knew how much Theresa was hurting... and was her constant companion. She spent countless hours on Theresa's lap, quietly providing comfort by her presence. And occasionally licking away some tears.

Theresa and Carlota have survived good and bad times together... they are a family.

Things Are Looking Good

I can't actually remember before my life with Theresa because when I met her I felt like that was when my life began. So let me start by telling you how we met…

I was with some ladies in a place where a lot of people were walking past. The ladies were patting me and people would stop and smile at me and scratch behind my ears.

One lady stayed for a looooooooong time, just looking at me and talking to me. She put a leash on me and we went for a nice walk. I got to smell lots of things and I stayed close to her because I didn't really know where I was and all I could see was people legs. I guess she got thirsty, because we stopped and she sat down at a table. I was a little tired, so I jumped on her lap and curled up. That seemed to make her real happy. She had something to drink, I had a little nap and things were looking good.

Then we went back to the place where we met. WHAT?!?! I thought I was nice and polite and well-behaved so she would like me and take me home. I didn't bark or bite anyone. I didn't pee or poop on anyone, or anywhere. What happened????

I was feeling pretty sorry for myself and a little bit mad at that lady. Then surprise, surprise… she came back! I got pretty excited, wagged my tail and looked at her, hopefully. She was carrying a lot of bags of stuff. One of the other ladies put the leash on me again. And the lady… her name is Theresa… and I started walking again.

We got to a big street and I saw something I needed to investigate. I took off running. At the same moment, Theresa stumbled and fell down. The leash came out of her hand. I heard a scream and I looked back for a second and Theresa was lying on the ground. All the stuff from her bags was on the ground too. She looked pretty unhappy and a lot mad. Some people were picking up her stuff and they helped her to stand up. She was hollering, "Carlota? Carlota! CARLOTA!" I didn't know that was my name. I did know I was probably in really big trouble. So I ran back to the place where I was before I met her. I figured that's where I'd end up anyway.

This is my most pitiful, pleading look.

I was just settling in for a nap when surprise, surprise (again) Theresa was standing in front of me with a serious look on her face. "So here you are," she said, "I have been looking all over for you." Then the biggest surprise, she picked me up and carried me under her arm. It wasn't too comfortable. I thought I better just be quiet, because Theresa was muttering stuff and I think it was angry stuff about me.

We got back to the place where… uh… our "accident" had occurred. I stayed verrrrrrry still under Theresa's arm. She gave a big sigh and said, "Now what? Where are my groceries?" And she started walking really fast and stomping her feet.

At her house… now MY house too… she gave another big sigh and sat down in a comfy looking chair. I jumped on her lap and thought I better give her some kisses. This had been a really bad day for her. She was hugging me and kissing me back. The doorbell rang. And it was this smiley family with all of Theresa's packages. They had figured out where she lived and brought them to her in new bags. She got the biggest smile on her face and just laughed and laughed.

Despite that rocky beginning, Theresa and I get along really well. We seem to understand each other. I sleep with her on the bed. She likes to lie on the bed and read, so I just cuddle right up next to her as close as I can get.

Everything was looking good until one day we moved to a new house. It was very big and really pretty. A man lived there. When I went over to him, he didn't seem too friendly. He didn't give me a scratch on the head like most people do. Uh-oh this might not be good, I thought.

So I went and jumped on the couch and he hollered at me. I got down on the floor and lay beside the couch. That night I jumped on the bed to sleep with Theresa, like always. He told me to, "Get off!" I gave him my sorriest, most pitifully pleading look. "Oh, all right then," he said. I was so happy, I wanted to make him happy, so I burrowed under the covers and lay on his feet to keep them warm. From then on he and I were very good friends.

Things were looking good again.

When he got sick I had to take care of him and Theresa. I gave them lots of kisses and cuddles and they gave me lots of hugs and sad smiles. One day he went away and never came back. Theresa cried a lot. I sat on her lap, real quiet. She just needed me to be close to her.

Now it's just Theresa and me again and things are looking good.

Driving Miss Daisy

Driving his truck on the main road around the north shore of Lake Chapala, Jim noticed a man and two boys walking on the opposite shoulder. A large dog trailed along a few paces behind them. Jim assumed the dog to be theirs. At that moment, a bus ploughed into the dog!

Jim stopped. He and the three pedestrians across the road all reached the dog at the same time. The man and his sons were vacationing locally. The dog was not theirs. The two men loaded the dog gently into the back of Jim's truck. The boys piled in the truck bed to be with the dog while the father, Francisco, accompanied Jim in the cab.

I feel just great!

The vet diagnosed the pregnant female with a broken pelvis, lacerations on her back legs, and significant blood loss. While she had no internal injuries, she did lose her nine puppies. When Jim picked her up two days later, she had been spayed, vaccinated, and was on the mend. The vet estimated her age at about one year.

He also learned that Francisco and his sons had left a note for him, together with 1,000 pesos toward the veterinary bill.

Driving Miss Daisy home, Jim had some anxiety about introducing her to his two large dogs, Fritz, the Weimaraner and the black and white long-haired mix named Dundee. He settled Miss Daisy into the casita where he made a bed for her and put out food and water. He sat with her for a long time as she lay on the bed. Finally, he went upstairs into the house.

At the sight of him, Fritz and Dundee went nuts! Jim turned to see Miss Daisy right behind him. He put leashes on the other two and gave everyone an opportunity to get acquainted. From the first instant, Fritz and Miss Daisy were friends. Fritz seemed to sense her vulnerability. Following Fritz's lead, Dundee warmed to her as well.

Jim and his wife, Patti, set about making special food for the malnourished Miss Daisy. She was so skinny her head looked too big for her body. None of this apparent debilitation stopped Miss Daisy from tearing around the yard, oblivious to her need to heal properly.

Francisco and his sons came to Jim and Patti's house to visit Miss Daisy and inquire after her recovery. Jim asked them if they wanted to take her home to Monterrey with them. "No, no," said Francisco, "we have five dogs."

Jim thought to himself, "And we now we have three dogs. This is the best thing I have ever done in my life.

I'm the Mom Now

I'm Miss Daisy. Jim gave me that name when he picked me up off the road. I'd been hit by a bus. I don't remember anything that happened before that. What I do remember is lying in a quiet place where I was in and out of sleep and people probed and stroked and hovered over me. I remember pain. It came and went...and came and went again.

People came and went, too. A man. Two young boys. Jim. The last time Jim came, I was feeling pretty good again so he took me home with him. He made a place for me and gave me food and water. I felt alone, anxious, and somehow empty inside. I was glad he was with me.

Something was missing. I lay there trying to remember where I lived, what happened before I got hit. Was I needed someplace? Then Jim left the room.

That won't do, I thought. And I went after him. That's when I met Fritz and Dundee. They seemed pretty anxious, too. Then Fritz got excited to meet me. We bonded right away. Pretty soon, Dundee let me know that he liked me too.

As Fritz and Dundee and I played together, I came to understand them better. I got this overwhelming urge to mother them, nurture them, take care of them. Jim and Patti take really good care of all three of us. No question about that! It's just that sometimes the guys need a little something more.

For example, Dundee had a hurt leg and he wore a bandage on it. I know it hurt him to have that bandage messed with, so I didn't allow it. I did notice sometimes that either Patti or Jim had put on a new bandage while I wasn't looking. They know I didn't approve. No one was allowed to hurt my Dundee.

Sometimes Fritz misbehaved. He's a boy! What do you expect? Patti will get the squirt bottle out to let him know he had to change his behavior. I jumped right in between them and scolded her about it. I'll tell Fritz whatever he needs to know.

I miss my boys so much.

Every now and then, I used to like to bring Jim a token of my appreciation for his kindness to me. I'd catch a critter trespassing in our yard where it didn't belong and put it where Jim could find it. The next thing I knew, he was scolding Fritz. I won't have that! I'll have to stop bringing him presents if he's going to fuss at my Fritz. I'm the only one who fusses at Fritz.

Today I'm feeling sad. My Fritz and Dundee have crossed the Rainbow Bridge. None of us saw it coming. I miss them so much! I really can't talk about it now. I'm just holding the memories for a while of the good life we shared together. You understand.

Ron's Legacy of Love

Bob and Ron moved to Lakeside for the second time in 2011. Ron was incurably ill and wanted Lakeside to be his final resting place. Along with them came their long-haired Chihuahua name Kookie.

Six weeks after they arrived, Kookie was diagnosed with congestive heart failure and died shortly after. Bob and Ron were comforted by the smile on her face as she took her last breath. They were both heart-sick and vowed to never have another dog in their family... until they ran into Gudrun Jones of Lakeside Spay and Neuter Ranch & Adoptions.

Gudrun really tried to convince them to visit the ranch... not necessarily for a dog... just to see the place. Bob and Ron both knew that if they went they would be tempted. And yet, neither one of them was ready to open his heart again.

After about three months, on a Sunday afternoon, the guys decided to go for a drive... which led them to the area of the ranch. They knew they were close when they heard the raucous barking of dogs. They saw about 80 dogs and lots of people, mostly chatting with and patting the cute and cuddly little fluffer puppies.

There was one medium-sized dog, alone in the back corner of a pen, on top of a doghouse. It looked interesting. Kind of a Heinz 57 type mix – some Pointer, some Weimaraner, some Labrador perhaps. Bob approached the pen and carefully stuck his hand through the wire. The dog immediately approached and started licking his hand. He touched the soft nose and fell in love with the silky black face and liquid brown eyes.

Ron was not as convinced. He said he didn't think they needed a dog, and not a big one. He wanted to consider their options.

Beautiful eyes and a heart full of love.

Ron finally decided that Bob would need a dog to soothe and console him when he was gone. So, within a few days, Ron relented. He loved Bob so much that he wanted this dog to be a symbol of his love after he passed on. He didn't anticipate the comfort that Matti, the beauty with the silky face and beautiful brown eyes, would provide to him in his final days.

Comfort and Joy

I love my humans… well, I only have one now. The other one was really sick and died. I sat next to him and lay beside him as much as I could. I'd growl if strange people tried to come too close to him. I knew he felt bad. His tummy hurt. And his heart hurt because he had to leave us.

Now it's just me and Bob. He really loves me and I really, really love him. He was sad for a long time and now he laughs more and we have more fun. I know when he's starting to feel sad again so I just bump up against him and jump and lick his face. That makes him laugh out loud. He talks to me and even if I don't know exactly what he's saying I really look at him and try to listen hard.

Once I tried to talk to him… we had been in the house all day and I really had to go outside. I waited and waited and finally I had to bark at Bob. He looked annoyed and said, "Not now Matti," and I felt bad so I went and lay down on the bed. I really, really had to go, I couldn't hold it any longer and… suddenly I pooped on the bed. I was so embarrassed and worried that Bob would be angry with me. I went to him and barked a lot and finally he followed me to the bed. He saw my mess and he didn't get mad! He told me he was sorry and how smart I was to try and tell him. Now he listens to me.

We play together lots. Bob gives me toys. I mostly chew them. I like to gnaw on stuff like my blankie. It has these wire-y things in it and I chew them and pull them out. Now it has a lot of holes in it and looks kinda raggedy, and I love it because it's really mine.

I can make Bob laugh… when we go to the beach, I take off and run as fast as I can. Like the wind. I just go faster and faster until I can't run any more and I stop and lay down, panting. Bob sits on a bench and just smiles and laughs. He calls me to share the water in his bottle. The other dogs go in the water to drink and swim and get sticks. Not me. Yuck, I don't like to get my paws wet.

I can make Bob laugh.

Bob really loves his computer. He can spend too much time with it and not enough with me. When I know he's had enough, I go and bump his hand with my nose. Then I sit and watch him. If he ignores me I try and jump in his lap. I weigh almost 50 pounds so he has to notice me then!

I gotta watch Bob all the time. There's only him and me now so we need to take care of each other. Ron and Kookie have crossed the Rainbow Bridge and one day it will be our turn. Until then we're going to be happy together.

Mexi-Can Menagerie on Phil's Hill

The mountain rolls into Lake Chapala below Phil Rowlatt-Smith's hilltop El Limon home in Jocotepec. Phil shares his life there with Phoebe and Luke, his two Canadian PLT (Poodle-Like-Thing) rescues, and Joker, his Mexican PLT rescue. Phoebe is the eldest. Noticing that she seemed lonely, Phil rescued Luke to keep her company. The three of them migrated to Lakeside in 2010.

I'm so glad you found me.   Hey, I got no complaints!

One November day in 2012, Phil heard Luke and Phoebe barking enthusiastically. He went to investigate and found that a tall, skinny white dog had wriggled under the gate onto the driveway. Phil began making inquiries in the neighborhood.

One friend had seen the dog wandering loose for at least two days, maybe more. Another had fed him for a couple of days. No one had heard of anyone looking for a dog.

As they all got acquainted, Phil noticed his new addition acted silly and was funny to watch. "It was pretty clear he'd never be the brightest bulb in any pack," Phil said. "The name Joker just came to me. It seemed perfect for him."

Phil had been thinking about getting a third dog anyway, and Joker made it easy for him by finding Phil. Off they went to the vet for neutering, a check-up, and shots. The vet guessed his age at about a year at that time.

Despite his goofy antics, Phil describes Joker as calm and docile. His personality is still developing. He's bigger than Phoebe and Luke, so he gets on his hind legs to be played with and puts his head on Phil's lap.

"Walking three dogs is twice as hard as walking two," Phil says. "I'm always having to untangle somebody."

Phil still keeps wood under the fence gate where Joker came in and hopes Joker will one day be too big to get out that way. That is likely to happen sooner than later as Joker is always first into the kitchen at mealtime. He looks for handouts between meals too.

"I'm glad he found me," says Phil. "I lucked out and I don't think he has too many complaints either."

The Joker is Wild

Where I live now I'm called Joker. I haven't always lived here. And no one ever really called me anything when I didn't. My Mom disappeared when I was still a young puppy. Puppies are cute, as you know, so finding food on my own wasn't too hard during the early months. My curls helped, too.

Before I knew it, I was no longer cute and tiny. I was tall and gangly and just didn't have the appeal to get regular food and water. I roamed the streets of Jocotepec for a long time just trying to stay alive. There were a lot of us on the street at that time. Winter was coming and the nights would be chilly. None of us had anyplace warm to sleep.

So I started off into the sunrise one morning and never looked back. I walked through the mountains looking for food and a friendly face. I was pretty tired by the time I got to this place where there were a lot of houses. Houses usually mean food. I started up the mountain.

I really got lucky! When I stopped at a house, I got fed. Sometimes I got fed more than once. Most of the houses had gates and fences around them, so I couldn't get in unless someone saw me and invited me.

One day I found a gate that had a space under it. I was pretty skinny then, so I just wriggled under it until I got inside. There were already two dogs living there, so I knew it was a dog-friendly place. They weren't too sure about me being there. Right away their huMan came out and said it was okay for me to stay.

Before you can actually live here full time, the huMan takes you to a special place to see a person he calls a vet. This vet person pokes and prods and makes human sounds like, mmmmm, and uh-huhhhhh, and gooooood. Then he sticks you a few times with a prickly thing. It all made me fall asleep and when I woke up, I felt pretty uncomfortable around my private parts.

It was all worth it because I'm still here. Sometimes my huMan leaves in his car. I always follow him because I want to go along and make sure he comes back. Phoebe and Luke don't seem concerned about that. Somebody has to be. He gives us food! What if he doesn't come back? Been there. Done that. No thank you.

Lovin' my toys in the morning.

Phoebe is the eldest. She's pretty laid back. Luke gets a little mouthy from time to time. He'll bark or snarl and expect a reaction from me. He doesn't get it. I just ignore him when he does that. Other times, when he wants to play, I'm on it. I love to play!

Phoebe and Luke are allowed on the bed at night. I'm not. No matter. I'm the biggest and I have my own bed on the floor. I sleep in it every night. In addition to that, I've found a sofa on the porch that I've turned into my favorite special place. I spend a lot of time there during the day.

The first thing every morning, before I go to my favorite sofa, I play with my toys.

My huMan has given me lots of toys because he knows that I love them and he wants to reward me for protecting our house.

In the evening, right before the sun goes down and darkness falls, Phoebe and Luke go off duty. They just tune out anything that goes on around our house when it's nighttime. I'm always on duty and bark when I sense danger. Even in the middle of the night...although my huMan seems less appreciative of my vigilance in the wee hours of the morning.

I just have to protect our house and keep everyone safe. As tired and weary as I was when I made my way up this mountain, it was worth the effort to find Phoebe and Luke and my new huMan who loves me. I want us always to be safe and together.

He's a Charlie

ill Orovan and his dog, Timmy, had been together for 16 years when Timmy crossed the Rainbow Bridge. Bill spends more time in Mexico now than he does in the U.S., so he decided to find a new furr-ever friend in the village of Ajijic where he shares his home with Bob Lewis.

Sitting in the plaza, as they often do in the evening, Bill saw a couple of really cute dogs wandering about. He befriended them and made some inquiries. As is often the case, they were not street dogs at all. They had homes with humans who cared for them.

Bill loves me very much!

Bill began a tour of the local shelters, which eventually led him to Anita's. As Bill struggled to make a real connection with the dog he had been invited to interview, he saw a wheat-colored, wire haired, mixed breed young dog standing on a nearby bench. They made eye contact and connected immediately. Bill brought him home.

Bill and Bob watched the little guy finding his way around the grounds and investigating his new environment for a couple of days. Finally, Bill declared, "He's a Charlie."

The vet estimated Charlie to be between eight months and one year old in June of 2013. His high-energy puppy behaviors are fun to watch. He feels protective of his new home and barks appropriately at new people he doesn't know...while running backwards from the interior gate. With one such backward quick-step, he ended up in the pool. Bob had to fish him out.

Bill says that Charlie is still sorting out images. He tried to jump on Bill whose image he saw in a full-length mirror, and bounced off the glass for his effort. Then he discovered his own image. When he paws at it, its paw meets his. Then he barks at himself as though his own image is a stranger in the room.

"He's a jumper," Bill says. "He jumped on my desk and walked across the keyboard a couple of times, so I took everything away. He still jumped on the desk." Maybe that's what being a "Charlie" is all about. High energy, jumping, running, playing, and entertaining the huMan who gave him a furr-ever home.

The Jumper

Hi! C'mon in! I'm Charlie and this is my house. Bill and Bob live here with me. It's a big place and it really keeps me busy. I spent my whole first day… all of it!… just sniffing the yard so I know exactly what's what out there. Then I had to check out the inside. I'm built a little close to the ground so sometimes I have to jump to see what I need to see.

Bill has a place where he keeps some of his stuff that seems to matter to him. I need to know what that's about, so I jump up there. It's not always smooth. One of his toys has little pieces that sink down when I step on them. Then another toy lights up and marks pop up on the lighted surface. I have little paws, so I'd rather not walk on those little pieces. I got Bill to move them just by jumping up there. He seemed to get it that those things were in my way.

I jump on Bob's lap sometimes when he's playing with his toys. He has a toy that's a lot like Bill's. When he tickles it with his fingertips another nearby toy lights up and gets marks on it, too. I sit with Bob looking at this toy trying to figure out what it's all about. I'm young yet. Given enough time I think I'll get it.

C'mon in! I've got a game for you, too!

Bill and Bob have given me a lot of cool stuff that I like to play with. I put them in a special place until we're ready to play. Then I take one at a time to Bill or Bob to throw. I run and get them and bring them back. It's so much fun! I knew Bill would really like a cool game like mine, too. So I get some of his toys, like shoes, sweaters, and other stuff, and put them on the shag rug in the middle of his bedroom. Then he gets to put them all back where I found them. I made the game up myself and I know he loves it!

Sometimes I feel like I need eyes in the back of my head. When humans come to visit I run backwards a lot. I have to watch them and make sure the property is safe. One time I was running backwards and ended up in water they keep in a huge blue hole in the back yard. Bob got me out. It seems a strange place to have a big blue hole full of water. The humans are able to dodge it unless they want to play in it on purpose. Here's the thing. I'm so happy to be here I don't want to sound critical. I just try to pay closer attention to where I'm stepping.

Bill loves me very much. So does Bob. I know I'll be here for a long time because they need me. Inside the house, there's a dog who looks just like me and does exactly what I do when I am looking at it! I bark at it and it still copies me. I have to keep an eye on it and make sure it stays on the other side of that surface so Bill and Bob will always be safe.

Serendipity

andy Wallin's travels have taken her from a small town in British Columbia, Canada, to a small town in Jalisco, Mexico. Maple Ridge to Riberas del Pilar was quite a journey. After visiting Lakeside several times, Sandy decided to make it home for her and her dog, Piper, in September of 2011.

They rented a house in Chapala and were settling in. Two weeks later, Sandy's landlady was desperately looking for a foster home for a dog her mother had rescued. Sandy and Piper decided it would be OK. And they began looking for a forever home for this Poodle-Like-Thing called Howard.

Howard did not like his photo taken… he would either turn or walk away at the critical moment. Sandy needed that photo to advertise his good looks, charm and availability. Words are just not enough to describe his goofy smile...how he can't quite close his lips with that under bite and his teeny, tiny teeth. That and his plaintive brown eyes just have to be seen.

He was also a bit skittish. Particularly when he heard thunder or cohetes… he would flatten himself into a small space, usually under a bed.

Sandy and Piper did not care for cohetes and thunder either. When Sandy heard of a house for sale in the quieter village of Riberas del Pilar, she looked at it and loved it. So, in December 2011, Sandy, Piper, and the temporary Howard, moved into their forever home.

One of the new neighbors was looking for a companion for her dog and Sandy told her about Howard. She was actually a bit surprised when the lady said she would like to take Howard. In fact, Sandy's first thought was, "I can't part with my Howard." And she didn't. He never became that companion.

Meant to be.

Howard is now an integral part of the family. Piper had been an only child for seven years. She had well-developed princess habits and expectations. She loved her life and was not enthusiastic about sharing it with this exuberant bundle of energy... in fact, he often makes her crazy. She just rolls her eyes and stomps off.

He has enriched their lives tremendously... probably Sandy's more than Piper's. They walk in the neighborhood and to the beach a couple of times a day. Howard always attracts attention and they have all rapidly assimilated into the culture of their neighborhood

Now in charge of security at the house, when Howard hears a noise in the night, he pops up, instantly alert... usually with one ear plopped over his head like a Donald Trump comb-over. He does a quick check of the premises, returns to the bed and flops down, instantly asleep.

Yes, sometimes things work out just as they are meant to be.

From Rags to Riches

I used to live on a roof with my brother… pretty cool, huh? We could bark at everyone who walked by and sometimes we'd scare people, just to see them jump… or scream (heh-heh). It was pretty fun. Some days it would get hot and we didn't get water so we didn't even have the energy to fool with people. We didn't get too much food either. And never treats. I guess we were poor.

One day a lady came and took me away. We went to a place that scared me. It didn't smell natural. It had a new smell I didn't recognize. People kept touchin' me and lookin' in my ears and mouth and pokin' me with skinny little sharp sticks. After the last poke, I fell asleep. Seemed like I was asleep for a looooooong time. When I woke up I was really sore… I mean really sore… uh, between my back legs, if you know what I mean.

Well that same lady took me to her house and we got along good. I would hear her talkin' to people about me… my name's Howard… and I would hear that a lot.

Finally I went to a house where there was another dog…. woooHOOOOOO… and some dog she was! Spoiled, stuck up, a real royal pain. She didn't want me to touch her stuff. She had a nasty growl and she could bare her teeth and turn real ugly. She wouldn't play with me so I'd jump in front of her and bow down and bark and stuff… oooooooooh, Missy Prissy would just roll her eyes and stomp off. Like I offended her or somethin'. Didn't bother me… I kinda enjoyed it (heh-heh).

It's a good thing the lady of the house was nice to me. She bought me my own toys and she talked to me and played with me and scratched my head just like I like it. I heard her talk about me a lot too. I figured we had a pretty good life.

One day we all moved to a real nice house. It's got lotsa places for me to sniff and dig and explore, inside and outside.

And there's this big blue water bowl. Whenever I get thirsty I just stroll over and lap up water… and remember the old days when there wasn't much water.

Are you ladies comin' ?

Our lady got really sick for a while. So I would sleep next to her… and that prissy Piper would lie in her fancy bed and watch me watch our lady. I stayed real quiet. Sometimes I slept. Mostly I just looked at her and let her stroke me. That seemed to make her feel better. She got well and now everything is back to our normal. Piper and I even tolerate each other… and keep our distance from each other.

We are back to taking our walks in the 'hood. I like to chase birds. I don't get too far away, though. I make sure I can always see our lady… whenever I hear her call my name, I stop what I'm doin' and get right back to her.

I try to be a gentleman 'cause I'm the man of the house. When guests come over to eat, I never beg at the table. I got a system. I just quietly put my head on their leg and give them my most pathetic look with my big brown eyes. That does the trick (heh-

heh). They laugh and give me a bite and I go and lie down. The lady rolls her eyes and laughs too.

When Piper and me eat we use the same bowl. Our lady puts it on the floor and says "lady first" and I wait patiently for my turn. After she regally strolls away, I eat slowly and savor every morsel. I don't make a mess. If something pops out of the bowl, I lick it up right away before anyone sees.

Life is good… you might say I've gone from rags to riches (heh-heh).

Teacher's Pets

Retired school teacher, Linda Samuels, moved from New York City to Ajijic in 1995. As she made friends and became active in the community, Linda noticed that often people would leave social gatherings to go home and feed their dogs or walk their dogs or care for their dogs. Never having had a pet of any kind in her life, Linda thought this pretty demanding, especially for retired people.

Soon, Linda began thinking about what it might be like to have a dog, and to save a dog from life on the streets. First, she asked her maid whether she would help by staying at Linda's house with the dog when she traveled. When the maid agreed, Linda went off to Anita's to find her first furry forever friend, Chula.

We do love our Queen Linda!

Chula was a wonderful dog who had serious health issues. Linda was inexperienced, so she found a dog whisperer who helped her. Chula was also diagnosed with Addison's disease and treated with steroids. Linda wanted something more holistic, so she sought out a homeopath who asked questions about Chula and about Linda and her personality. Soon the steroids were out of Chula's system and herbal treatment for the Addison's cured that as well.

Chula was about two years old when Linda found Guapo, a tiny white puppy wandering the streets of Chapala, fending for himself. He was sick, weak, and less than six months old. He was so tiny Linda could hold him in her hand. The first thing he did when Linda brought him home was go to the yard and eat dirt. It was what he was accustomed to eating.

Homeopathy got Guapo through several illnesses and Linda nursed him to a healthy weight with special food she prepared for him herself. "He went from pauper to prince in a very short time," Linda says of Guapo. "He's a very finicky eater and turns his nose up at anything that isn't fresh-cooked." At age 13, Guapo is the picture of health and a testament to loving care.

After 15 years together, Chula crossed the Rainbow Bridge early in 2013, leaving Guapo behind. As Linda watched Guapo grieve for Chula, she wanted to find a companion for him. She went to Anita's to find a dog two or three years old. "A puppy is too much work at this time in my life," Linda said. At the same time, Dulce came into Anita's with her leg in a cast. She had been hit by a car and the person fostering her could no longer keep her. So Linda left Anita's with seven-month-old Dulce and a sense that God had put them together.

Linda's support network extends around her Ajijic neighborhood as her gardener's children have grown up with the dogs and love to take them for walks. Linda's maid is family, the surrogate huMom to Chula, Guapo, and now Dulce. "Having had dogs in my life now for all these years has also been good for my growth as a person and for my own spiritual development." Clearly, it has been good for the dogs as well.

Prince Guapo

How do you do. My name is Guapo. I am a prince. I have not always been royalty. That is, I was not born into it. Rather I was groomed for it by my precious Queen Linda. I shall tell you about it.

I came into the world a tiny fur ball with no mother, no father, and no sisters or brothers. My first memories are of waking up alone on the streets of Chapala. My memory is poor because I rarely ate any food, so I was barely conscious in those days. I was too little even to be noticed by anyone. When scraps appeared on the street, the bigger dogs all got to them first. There was dirt around the trees along the sidewalks and that would fill me up when I was just too weak to walk. Water was scarce as well.

One day as I was standing on the street, too dizzy to walk, Queen Linda walked by and saw me there. She scooped me up and I curled into the palm of her warm hand. Doggie Heaven, I thought. I have died and gone to Doggie Heaven.

The next thing I remember is being licked on the face by a full-grown dog who I later learned was named Chula. Chula let me know I was safe here in the palace of Queen Linda. At first I wasn't so sure. I was weak and hungry. There was good dirt in the palace garden and I helped myself. I explored the palace until I found a tiny room where I curled up behind a door. Because I liked my first taste of Doggie Heaven I just stayed quiet and waited for the warmth to come again. It did. I was cupped in Queen Linda's hand once more.

Weeks passed as Queen Linda prepared special food for me and I grew into a strong young prince. Chula became my loyal subject. She played with me and kept me amused. Sometimes one of my other subjects would offer me something to eat that was beneath my discerning taste. Of course, I had to decline. I could not have my subjects thinking I would eat just anything.

I AM a prince.

Chula was my loyal subject for many years. I grew to love her very deeply. Before she crossed the Rainbow Bridge, I commanded her to wait in the grass there for me and Queen Linda. When she was finally gone, I grieved in my own royal way.

Queen Linda is as wise as she is loving. Young Dulce has come to the palace to live. Trust me, she is not princess material. It is my job now to show her how best to serve me.

A Little Sugah Goes a Long Way

My name is Dulce...and Ah am sweet as sugah, Sugah. Aftah all Ah been through, I can't be any othah way. Ah came out of the worst mess you can imagine and right into the lap of luxury here with Sweet Linda, who is sweetah even than Ah am.

Ah was livin' on the streets as a young girl just tryin' to stay alive when outta nowheah, somethin' just slammed right into me and threw me up in the air and smack back down on the ground again. Ah couldn't walk. Ah could barely breathe. Ah just laid there.

And Ah AM sweet as sugah.

Some kind folks found me and took me to the doctah where Ah got a cast on mah leg. That was awkwahd. Ah stayed for a time with a lovely woman who took very good care of me, and then she had to leave the country. She took me ovah to Anita's. Anita is a sweet woman with about a million dawgs waitin' for homes. Ah knew ah'd be thea for a long time, what with my broken leg and all. Honey, Ah was so wrong!

Sweet Linda walked in almost at the same time Ah did. She was lookin' for a little friend for her Guapo. That crazy dawg thinks he's a prince! What a hoot! I humah him because he's just real good to me. Mah leg healed right away and Linda takes me walkin' on the malecon to help me strengthen it. I love everybody we see down thea. Everybody is just so nice to me.

Ah can hardly believe my good fortune. Ah'm pretty sure some of it is because Ah'm just so sweet to everybody, so Ah'll keep doin' that. Even with "Prince" Guapo.

Survivors

Over a 10-year period, Beth enjoyed visiting her parents in Lakeside. Finally, in 2009, she decided to buy a one-way ticket, pack up a few belongings and her beloved pure-bred Cocker Spaniel, Benny, and take an extended vacation. She came from Canada, where *winters* can be extended! It wasn't long before she had fallen in love with the area. Benny had found his bliss.

Shortly after Beth and Benny had settled into their house, they were robbed… at gunpoint. It was a horrifying experience for both pf them. The thieves took some things… more tragically; they robbed Beth and Benny of their confidence and sense of security. With the help and support of Beth's parents and her many dear friends, she and Benny relocated to a house with large guards and gates. Over time they regained their confidence and still love Lakeside as much as ever.

Benny was ruling the roost at her house and her parents' place. Always the only dog, he got all the attention he needed, and more. Their lives were practically perfect. Having another dog would only complicate things. All her friends even said so.

She was buying Benny's food at the animal shelter store when she stopped to look at the photos of dogs needing homes. She wasn't seriously looking, just curious. There was one face that caught her attention. It was just a puppy, only three months old. It had a wistful melancholy about it… a depth of feeling. Something told her there was a story behind those mournful eyes. When she heard why he was up for adoption, Beth's heart ached.

Not wanting to upset Benny's life, nor cause the shelter dog more sadness, Beth arranged to have the dog come for a visit. After spending an afternoon together, two things were clear… that the puppy adored Benny (he tolerated the puppy)… and the puppy loved to lick toes.

We thrive together.

Beth saw an angelic quality about the year-old Cocker Spaniel and Dachshund mix. He had survived trauma and so had Beth. They had a connection. He would be a sweet addition to her family. To honor his Mexican heritage, she named him Benito.

Grateful

I was walking on the mountain. It was a clear, quiet night. I was sniffing in some bushes. Boom! I looked for my sister. She was lying still on the grass. I went over to sniff her. She wasn't breathing. A mean man kicked me away and was shouting. I looked for my huMan. He was lying very still on the ground too. He had something like a leash wrapped around him. I lay down next to him as far under his leg as I could get. He was breathing. I stayed very still. The horrible man went away.

We stayed like that until it got light. Then my huMan wriggled and struggled and got his leash off. He picked me up and we walked down the mountain. We were both shaking from fear. When we got home, everyone was crying and hugging us. I felt frightened and nervous. I was glad to be alive.

My human family took me to meet a nice lady. She had an old dog named Benny. He's too old to play much. I really liked the lady. She's pretty and she has really nice toes. I like to lick toes and hers are especially tasty. She laughed and scratched my head.

I stayed at her house when my family went home. I thought they would come to visit me. They never did. I'm grateful that they found me a safe place to live.

My new huMom is named Beth. Isn't that a soft and gentle name? Just like her. She calls me Benito… and she says it with such love. We have a unique connection. She rubs my tummy in a special way and I smile at her to let her know I like it and how much I appreciate her… I even show my teeth. She has suffered trauma in her life and so have I. We're grateful to have each other to love.

Sometimes she and Benny and I go in the car. Because he's older than me, he lays down on the back seat. I think the old guy sleeps back there. I'm so excited to see everything that I sit in the front with Beth. I put one paw on the front and one on the door and just look around. I want to keep my eye on what's going on around us.

Thank you Beth... and Benny.

Benny's lived with Beth for a long time. He came with her to Mexico. They flew in the air! He's a smart old guy. I listen to everything he tells me. I want to absorb all his wisdom. When I lie down beside him and snuggle, he just sighs and doesn't move much.

We both like to take sunbaths... especially in the afternoon. Sometimes we go with Beth and she jumps in some water and flaps around. Me and Benny?... we just lounge on the special sun couches and watch her.

I have lots of energy so I'm always exploring new places around the house and the yard. Every night, I take a run as fast as I can, in and out and all around… just to make myself tired. When we all get into Beth's bed, Benny and I cuddle up to her. She watches TV. I watch it too. Benny sleeps. I have to really focus because there's always stuff moving. My favorite channel is Animal Planet because there are lots of shows about dogs and other animals. Sometimes, when I hear those dogs bark, I look behind the TV. They must run away quick, because I never see them.

Beth uses a clicky thing to turn off the TV. That's my signal to give her one more adoring look and then hop down to the floor. I sleep under the bed where it's safe and dark and I'm not afraid. I dream about my old family… and Beth and Benny… and how grateful I am to be here with them.

After the Star Has Gone Out, Then Cometh the Moon

Artist, Antonio Cardenas, was born in Ajijic and has lived there all of his life. He has also had dogs all of his life. His last dog was named Estrella, which means star. Estrella was with Antonio for ten years before crossing the Rainbow Bridge.

One morning in November of 2012, Antonio was walking on the road with a friend. He saw a beautiful female mixed-breed Lab. Their eyes met and she fell into step with Antonio and his friend. She was clearly malnourished, so as they got closer to Antonio's home, he stopped to buy her some food.

The next day Antonio set out with his new four-legged house-guest to try and find her owner. When they walked onto the grounds of the Lake Chapala Society, the dog immediately reacted to a man whom she obviously recognized. Jumping and pulling on the leash as she was, it was clear to Antonio that he had to be the owner.

"Where did you find the dog?" the man asked?

"Running all over town. Everyone said she belongs to someone."

"That's my dog," the man said. "And you can have her if you want her. Her name is ShaSha."

It was clear to Antonio from the way ShaSha looked that she had been away from her owner for a long time. Antonio didn't ask any more questions. He was happy to take her home and nurture her back to a healthy weight.

ShaSha became Luna (moon), following Antonio's lost "star." Although Antonio does say he named her too quickly. He named her before he learned what a flirt she is, with people and with other dogs. Perhaps Coqueta would have been a more appropriate name.

Let's go for a walk, Antonio.

Antonio and Luna enjoy walks together along the lakeshore and in the mountains, usually three times a day. Antonio has no idea how old she is. He just notices that when they are not walking or interacting together in his gallery/home, she is fast asleep.

Luna has filled out into the picture of health now. Her new life in her new home clearly agrees with her.

Starry, Starry Night

I'm Luna and I'm beautiful. All the other dogs say so. People say so, too. We are all about beauty where I live. My Antonio is an artist. Need I say more?

I have a great life with Antonio. He understands me. For example, he knows what I like to eat. Canned food is my favorite. I also favor some human foods, too, just not ham. I won't eat ham. I don't eat kibble, either.

Speaking of food, some old habits die hard. I lived on the street for a while before I found Antonio and flirted with him all the way to his house. When a lady lives on the street, she is sometimes reduced to eating whatever's there. It's so familiar to me even now that Antonio has to pull me up short sometimes because… well… I'm eating whatever is there on the street.

My favorite time of day is morning! Antonio and I walk down the street to the lake and then we walk along the malecon. On the way back, we go right to the edge of the water. He'll throw a stick way out into the water. I go get it, swimming sometimes if I have to, and bring it back to him so he can throw it again. He seems to like throwing the sticks so I make sure he gets to do it as often as he wants.

Sometimes I meet friends by the lake. There's a very handsome black dog I hang out with. I don't know his name. It doesn't matter, really. I just sidle up to him. We play together in the lake and sometimes we go to the park, too.

When we play in the park, I love to nuzzle the human puppies who play there too. They have only two legs and they're so cute when they run up to me and put their tiny paws on my face. It makes me feel so good I wag all over. I like to play with regular puppies, too.

Yes, I am quite the coquette.

Mornings aren't the only time we walk. Whenever I want to go for a walk, I just go to where Antonio is, make funny faces at him, and move my head in a way that lets him know it's time to go. I've trained him well in that regard.

We get so much exercise during the day, that when we aren't at the lake, in the park or hiking the mountains, I can usually be found taking a long, sound siesta. I love to sleep because when I sleep, I dream. And when I dream I dream about Antonio and how lucky I feel that we're together in my forever home.

Whatever Lola Wants...

Rhoda Wamoldt has lived in Lakeside since 2000, so by 2008 she had been long involved in various volunteer activities in the community. One such activity put her in a booth at the annual Chili Cook-Off across the aisle from a booth sponsored by The Spay and Neuter Ranch.

The Ranch displayed several large photographs of dogs that needed forever homes. As Rhoda worked, she kept noticing one picture from which the dog seemed to be staring longingly at her. Perhaps the dog reminded her of her friend's schnauzers who Rhoda used to look after in Panama when her friend traveled. Perhaps it was because that very friend, Beverly, was now visiting Rhoda and her husband, Jim.

Rhoda, you and Jim need to just stay calm, okay?

Jim had been in the military for 33 years and always believed it was unfair to have a dog to uproot, move around, and leave for long periods. Beverly went to work on him, reminding him that they weren't in the military anymore and that a dog would be a wonderful and loving companion to them both. Finally, Jim conceded.

The following Monday Rhoda took a leash to the Ranch. The name of the dog in the photo was Lola and she did just what Rhoda hoped she would. She came right to the fence and looked at her expectantly. They went directly to the vet for a check-up and shots. He estimated her age at about a year and a half.

Lola is the perfect name for her because whatever Lola wants, Lola gets. Rhoda gives her a cookie and then Lola goes to Jim and licks her chops. She accompanies him to the kitchen for a bacon strip. She goes to the spa every three weeks for hair and nails. Lola shuns large dogs and small children. She ignores everyone else. She's very aloof.

Jim and Rhoda eat only at restaurants where dogs are welcome. Lola finds a shady spot and lays there, unmoving, until it is time to leave. They travel with her everywhere. She is always welcome at B&B's and in the homes of friends who have dogs.

Once a friend came to visit who had a very small dog. The dog was frightened and tried to hide under a bed. It couldn't quite make it. Lola went into a closet in the same room and the little dog came in and lay down beside her.

"Lola never barks," Says Rhoda, "We had her for a year before the neighbors even knew she was here. I don't think there could ever be another Lola."

Lola Creates the Life She Loves With the Loves of Her Life

My name is Lola, and I cannot tell you how delighted I am to be living with Rhoda and Jim. My life had a lovely beginning with a very fine couple. Sadly, they had to leave Ajijic suddenly because of his health. It all came on so quickly that there was no time to make arrangements for yours truly.

The interview process for their replacements was not a long one. I have a good sense of humans who fit well into my needs and my routine. I chose Rhoda without hesitation. Jim was a bonus. What a fabulous guy!

The first thing I had to do after I settled into their lovely home with them was get them trained properly. Local people trainer Art Hess came twice a week for six weeks. Jim and Rhoda learned quickly. We're all on the same page now and I take them everywhere with me.

My preference is to work smarter, not harder. I can protect our home just fine because I can see who comes to the door from my strategic place in the living room. If I know the person, I allow Rhoda to open the door without voicing any concern. If I don't know the person, I bark. When Rhoda says, "Thank you, Lola." I know she is heeding my warning and has things under control.

I'm very particular about certain things. For example, I enjoy walking with Rhoda along the malecon. It's quite lovely, and I especially like the little dogs who sometimes play there. It does concern me if the bigger dogs get too close to them. I don't want the little ones to get hurt, so I let the big dogs know to move on.

I enjoy walking along the beach as well. I do not enjoy getting wet in any way for any reason. I do not play in the lake. I do not run into the ocean when we go to the beach. And I certainly don't go out in the rain. I was on the patio when a few drops of rain fell just the other night. I went inside immediately and got under the dining room table. One can't take too many precautions when it comes to water.

Spa day? Of course. Why not?

Speaking of rain, we do have some loud thunderstorms here. I love listening to the rain and the thunder while I'm napping. Sometimes we can hear the fireworks from the church in the village. They don't really bother me either. Ours is really a pretty serene house.

One thing that does get my attention has to do with something Rhoda and Jim watch on the big screen they keep in front of their favorite chairs. I can see little people going back and forth across the screen really fast. They seem to slide more than run. They have long sticks in their hands. They chase a tiny black dot and hit at it with their sticks.

I have no idea what that's all about. What I do know is that Rhoda and Jim get very excited watching it. I'm constantly running to one of them or the other to see if I can help in some way. Just when I think I've got them calmed down, their arms are up in the air and they're howling again. If it keeps up, I may need to get Art back over here.

Another thing I'm very particular about is my food. I have to be. I have Lupus. Rhoda is such a dear. She makes all of my meals from fresh foods, rice, barley, grain, raw chicken, beef, and salmon. I feel so loved and I let her know every chance I get how much I appreciate her.

Jim, of course, gives me whatever I want in the way of Barky's Beggin' Strips, and cookies that come from a place in San Juan Cosala. I know I'm very special to him, just as he is to me.

When I'm at the spa, or just lounging here at home, I often re-flect on how very lucky I am to have chosen these two wonderful people to share my life.

I Love Lucy

When Julius Mann came to Chapala from Chicago in 2012 following his retirement, he had never had a dog in his life. He stayed in a casita in Chapala Haciendas where the owner cared for several street dogs on her property. Even though he'd never had any close encounters with dogs, Julius really had no objection to the dogs being around. In fact, he kind of liked the idea.

Almost immediately, a little dog named Lucy started to show up at the door to his casita every morning. When he emerged, she trotted off behind him wherever he went. When he returned at the end of the day, she was waiting for him.

I don't know what I'd do without Lucy

Eventually, he let her into his casita. Wherever he sat, she sat beside him on the floor, or dozed at the foot of his bed. Lucy got to know his car and sat beside it before he left the property. Once, when he went out to retrieve some papers, she got into the car and wouldn't come out...for three hours.

Finally one day Julius quietly quietly slipped away and drove two kilometers toward the Guadalajara-Chapala Highway en route to the dentist. Julius was pretty sure Lucy wouldn't enjoy the dentist's chair. When he got to the highway, he stopped his car and waited for a break in the traffic. As he waited Julius heard a panting sound and heavy breathing. When he got out to investigate, Lucy was beside his car, tail wagging, so happy to see him. He scooped her inside and went on his way.

That is the last day Julius and Lucy were apart. He takes her everywhere he goes. Julius says he is a different person as a result of knowing Lucy Girl. He considers her his best friend and looks forward to enjoying many happy years with her as his constant companion.

Pay Attention, Big Guy!

I had a good life in the Haciendas. Sra. Habenia took good care of all of us...sometimes as many as eight of us...and I ate good, played all day, and slept really well with my buddies. Even though Sra. Habenia was good to me, I wasn't really really exceptional to her, you know? I remember one time in my life when I felt really special to somebody. It's a feeling. I can't tell you anything about the person any more. I just remember how it felt. I wanted that again. I really wanted to feel loved in an exclusive way. Maybe I'd been an only puppy. I can't explain it. I just needed somebody for my own.

One day this really big guy came to our place. He had a warm voice and was very happy. When I got close to him, I felt something tingly so I always wanted to be close to him. He didn't get it. I sat in front of his door every morning and he seemed really glad to see me. Then he'd leave and I didn't get to go. Finally, finally, finally! He let me into his little house and I slept by his bed. I knew then that he felt the same thing I felt. Okay, maybe not yet.

So then I got in his car to let him know I could go with him wherever he was going. I would be a special friend to him. I was a great companion. I love people. I don't bark. I certainly won't run away. If I could just get him to take me with him one time, he would know. He wandered off again. I sat there for a long time waiting for him to come back so we could go wherever he was going. He didn't come. Finally, I got out of the car. He was a tough one to get through to. Sigh...

One day he got in the car before I could join him and drove off. He forgot me! I knew I'd have to catch up with him so I could go and show him what a great team we'd make. I ran as fast as I could! I ran and ran on my short legs until his car finally stopped.

I put my paws on the car. I was panting so hard I couldn't bark.

Whew! He was a tough one to get through to.

How would I let him know I was there? I guess he finally felt the same thing I felt between us because he came around the car, picked me up, and put me inside. He finally got it. Now we're never apart. I've heard him say, "I never had a dog in my life and now I don't know what I'd do without Lucy." Lucy. I love the way he says my name. And I love him. Forever.

Angels Come in All Shapes and Sizes

S teve and Lana Coffman were living across the street from La Paloma Bed and Breakfast in the spring of 2011. When Steve was asked to "babysit" the B & B for a little while in June, it gave him something useful to do. He noticed even then that his energy was low. What he did not know was that he had cancer.

When he arrived at La Paloma, Steve got the story about a little dog that was sleeping outdoors in the gardener's shower. All he had to do was feed her. Someone would come to walk her. She was there temporarily because there was a virus spreading through the Animal Shelter and they could not accept her. Steve took one look at her and realized that even if they could accept her, she was so old no one would adopt her. As time passed, no one came to walk her either.

Steve found a length of rope and the little dog jumped up ready to go for a walk. The two of them canvassed the neighborhood for more than two hours looking for the owner. Later, because of his fatigue, Steve asked Lana if she would walk the dog. Lana said, "I'm afraid if I walk her, I'll just walk her right home." Steve said that would be all right.

In their rented home, the little dog became "Lola," after Lana's mother, Lolita. Every time Steve sat down, or went to bed, Lola curled up on his lap and cuddled into his abdomen. When he went anyplace in the house or outside, Lola was beside him.

Steve went to the doctor late in June of 2011 about an ear problem, and talking a bit of fatigue. The blood draw revealed a white count too high for an ear infection. While putting cream on a skin rash, Lana discovered hard lumps in Steve's abdomen and they returned to the doctor. A biopsy revealed lymph nodes filled with cancer. While the testing was being done to select the proper course of treatment, Steve was deciding whether he was going to do any treatment at all. Lola lay in his lap, leaning against his abdomen, as he contemplated his choices. Two weeks later, Steve began an aggressive regimen of chemotherapy for lymphatic lymphoma. After the first treatment, Lola never got on Steve's lap again.

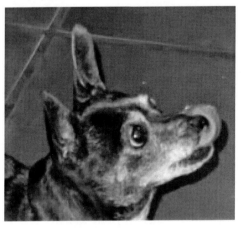

That looks yummy!

The Heart of Healing

Steve was sick when I found him. Sick and really tired, too. I've been around this village a long time and I know sickness when I get near it. Yes. Steve was sick.

I was drawn to him from the last place I'd been needed. A few years before, I came upon a woman who was ailing in her heart. She was old, like I am now, and she had nobody. I went inside her house with her one time and she took a liking to me. I stayed with her, curled up against her ailing heart every night. We spent many nights together as her heart beat slower and slower. Late one night when it was very dark and quiet, I felt her heart beat for the last time. Then it was still.

I climbed off the bed and waited by the front door. When it opened, I left. My work there was finished.

I roamed through the village looking for the next person I could help. The moment I started up Steve's street, I knew someone there really needed me. I found my way into La Paloma Bed and Breakfast where I had a chance to rest and get some food.

Of course, not all of us street dogs get taken to a safe place until someone chooses us for a forever home. I got taken to one of those places, even though I knew I shouldn't go. As it turned out, I had to leave right away because there was sickness there, too. So back to the B & B I went and that was fine with me. I was needed there.

The first time I met Steve, I knew he was the one I had to take care of. His sickness was in his belly, so I sat on his lap and laid against it every chance I got. Every time he sat down, I was on him.

Steve didn't live at the B & B. I figured that out when Lana, his wife, came from someplace else to walk with me. She was very sweet and I loved her. Steve loved her too… I could tell. I had a lot of work to do with Steve and I knew Lana would help me.

I knew Steve was the one I had to take care of.

One day Steve went with Lana to a vet for humans. They seemed very concerned when they came home to the house we all shared across the street from the B&B. I continued to sit on Steve's lap and curl up against his belly every time he sat down, which was often because he was tired a lot.

Steve and Lana left one day and when they came back, Steve seemed better. I noticed when I sat on his lap that the sickness wasn't as bad. In just a day or two, it was gone. Steve didn't need me to sit on his lap anymore, so I didn't. I still don't.

You just never know about these things. I'm with him wherever he is in our new house. I go to the store with him. We walk together. And when he's outside, I'm either sunning myself on the patio, or keeping an eye on things from my chaise.

My Steve is healthy now and my job is to keep him that way.

Spectacular Teddi

Nick and Robin Brewer moved to Lakeside from Albuquerque in 2004. By 2007, both of the dogs who had moved with them had crossed the Rainbow Bridge. While at a social function one evening, they sat next to Gudrun Jones, co-founder with Diane Hazen of the Lakeside Spay and Neuter Ranch and Adoptions. Gudrun invited Robin to the Ranch to meet some of the dogs who were awaiting forever homes.

Gudrun had a particular Tibetan Terrier-Standard Schnauzer mix in mind. She had been at the ranch for a month. When Robin saw Teddi for the first time, she was running in the sun with her fur flying. "She was spectacular!" Tibetan Terriers are raised by monks. They are never sold. Rather they are given as gifts and said to be very spiritual. Nick agreed that Teddi was, indeed, spectacular and that she should have a forever home with them.

Thanks, Nick. I'd love to have a treat.

Teddi's full name is Teddi Bear and, when seen in motion, clearly the name fits. Teddi moves like a grizzly on all fours. Nick runs with her on the carretera, and in the mountains. She is not aggressive at all. She does, however, defend herself much like a bear. When under attack, she rears up on her hind legs, grabs her opponent by the neck, and smacks it down. Nick calls her "Ninja Dog."

"She's also very laid back," says Robin. "She walks away before people finish petting her." At the same time, she's a wonderful watch dog who barks when strangers approach. Nick and Robin feel very secure with Teddi in the house.

Ninja Dog

I had a rough start in life, alone on the streets of Chapala, my hair down to the ground. I got caught unawares once… and a little while later I had a litter of puppies. I don't know what happened to them. I only know that I wasn't able to care for them for very long. Food was scarce. Sometimes…okay, a lot of the time, I ate rocks. Ruined my teeth. You see, I'm a big, independent girl, so people were naturally afraid of me. Sometimes they threw rocks at me when I was foraging for food. So I picked up the rocks and ate them.

I got very good at catching birds. I was, and still am, a stealth huntress, stalking my prey so it won't fly away before it's within reach. Then I'd knock it down as it took off and eat it in three bites. To tell you the truth, old habits die hard. When I moved into Nick and Robin's, they had a sparrow problem. Now they don't. It's part of my job, protecting the property and keeping it clear of pesky little birds, possums, and rats.

I'm watchin' you, birdie!

Robin and Nick are great people and I love them with all my heart. Because of my earlier experience with humans on the streets of Chapala, I'm a little wary of other people. I check them out carefully when they come through the door. Once I'm sure they're okay, I accommodate them. I have a bed in every room and a dog door at every entrance to our hacienda style house. I'm never far away when other people are here, and I make sure I can get to Nick and Robin in a flash.

I love to run with Nick in the mornings and I love to get back home so I can be sure everything's all right. Nick and Robin appreciate me and I know it. It helps them if I let them know when I want a treat, so I raise my paw. Then they know. As soon as I get my treat, I walk away. I'm not one to be pesky. I have a good life here and a good home. I intend to keep it that way.

Jet-Setters

Clive and Lily are passionate about rescuing dogs… and cats. They cannot imagine life without animals around. They've lived all over the world and have become serial adopters. When they look for a house to rent or buy, the number one item on the must have, non-negotiable list is pet-friendly.

Clive served on the Board of the Humane Society in the Bahamas. Of course, that position gave him the opportunity to have his pick before dogs were advertised for adoption.

Clive and Lily's life in the Bahamas was idyllic… well, except for the difficulties in a neighbor's marriage. Their pets had become bargaining chips and pawns. The three pedigreed dogs were spending a lot of time at Clive and Lily's house to stay out of the fray. When the marital assets were divided, Clive and Lily got custody of the elderly dogs. Everyone was happy.

Their house became home to so many lucky dogs.

For example, there was a black Lab-Great Dane mix who came from the shelter, joined the household, and was known as Harry Potter.

Then there was Skinny… she lived around the local Kentucky Fried Chicken outlet. She was a tough one to convince to leave that life. She quickly realized she had made the right choice.

Lisa was a Chow-Border Collie combination who loved to mother everyone in site.

And others passed through Clive and Lily's home, enjoying a life of bliss and contentment.

In 2005, when it was time to retire, Clive and Lily moved to Ajijic, where they had visited often and had purchased a home. This was a major move, involving 13 suitcases, two cats, four dogs, and the two humans. At the time, there was an embargo on transporting animals out of the Bahamas. Not to be deterred, Clive and Lily rented a private airplane to transport everyone!

We've found our home.

Over time, the dogs were crossing over the Rainbow Bridge. Clive and Lily often saw dogs from the Lakeside Animal Shelter being walked. One caught Clive's eye… a yummy looking chocolate Lab. He went to the shelter and waited for its return. He met Chocolate and took him home.

Chocolate was a tough guy. Having spent too long on the streets of Chapala he had a definite mean streak. He needed a lot of loving and nurturing to fit smoothly into the family. He is now called Bruno, which seems more appropriate to his nature.

One night a friend rang the doorbell. In her arms was a quivering, three-month-old English Setter wannabe who needed a home. The puppy jumped directly into Clive's arms and Clive said, "I think you've found it."

Paco had come home too.

Once a Bad Boy, Always a Bad Boy?

OK, OK... I know you mighta heard some stuff about me... and not very good stuff... like I'm mean... aggressive to other dogs... and I got a big bark. Some humans even say I was "incorrigible" whatever that is. Yeah, I was the chocolate terror.

Now the main thing you gotta understand is I was all that. If you hadda live on the streets of Chapala, you might be "incorrigible" too. I mean, I never went to charm school or nothin'. I just did what came natural to survive.

My education all started when a guy met me at the shelter and took me home. Another coupla dogs were there. One was called Lisa. She was real old... and nice to me. She was tellin' me stuff I had to learn... like I hadda pee in the garden, not in the house.

It took a while, four different trainers, and a really nice place to live before I could stop bein' such a bully. Now I can be the real me. I feel safe, secure... and, OK, loved... so I became the gentleman I was always meant to be.

It's important to know what to do. We get a lotta visitors and our humans go on trips sometimes. When they're away, we still get our walks at the same time and a lady comes and stays with us to make sure we get fed and loved. I'm always on my best behavior, with everyone.

There's one small problem... in the form of a cat named Sophie. That chick is wild. She attacks me! For no reason. I'm a big guy and she's little, and as a gentleman, I can't fight back. I just go to my crate for some privacy and quiet time. I wish it had a door.

Now that I know how to behave I get along with everybody

here… well, except for that Sophie thing that I just told you about. I got a good friend named Paco. We're runnin' buddies in the house. Kinda like my old days with my pack on the streets… just more civilized now, ya know?

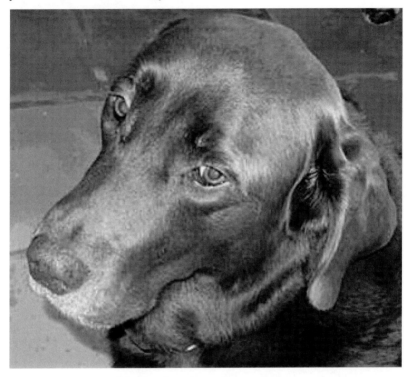

Yeah, the chocolate terror.

I love goin' in the car to this dog park where we play with other dogs. I'm good at chasin' a stick and bringin' it back. Oh yeah, and we go to the lake too. I really don't care much for gettin' wet so I let Paco do all the fetchin' from the water. Once my ankles are wet, I've had enough of that nonsense.

I'm slowin' down… just a bit, as I get older. My hips are startin' to hurt and I gotta take medicine for that. I also take medicine for my allergies… sneezin' is so unattractive. And not too refined.

Before I go, here's one more funny thing I gotta tell ya… remember I am a gentleman… most of the time. I have one little thing I do to lady visitors… especially the ones in short skirts. I just walk over and flip up their skirt with my nose! Humans seem to like that trick. The ladies act surprised and everyone laughs. Just part of my charm.

OK, I gotta go, 'cause it's Paco's turn to tell his story.

Latin Lover

Hey... it's me... Paco, the Latin Lover of the house. I loooooooooove people, especially their legs, if you know what I mean.

I came to this house as a very small pup so all of my memories are of here, and of this family... Bruno, my best amigo, and Clive and Lily, our amazing humans. Oh... and the gata... her name is Sofeeah... that's how you say her name correctly, in Spanish. She's not as bad as Bruno says. She's just a cat... and she's on medication... homeopathic... I don't actually know what that means so I can't 'splain it to you.

With the exception of Sofeeah, everyone in the family is fabulous and my life is practically perfect. I mean there was just one time when Lily got very sick and I was so worried. I lay by her side and gently licked her hand and when she moved I looked up to make sure she was OK. She tells me I was a good nurse because I gave her undivided care and attention. Again, sorry I can't 'splain that, you probably know what it means, right? And that's the only bad memory I have.

Our life is so full... me and Bruno... we're a pretty good team. I keep him away from the big blue water in the back yard... he doesn't like to get wet, ya know. We go in the car, with our heads out the windows to feel the breeze, and we play at the dog park or the lake. I swim out to get the sticks in the lake because, I hate to say it, so I'll whisper... Bruno's too old.

We actually do everything together, Bruno and me. We share our meals... he eats first, then me... and when I finish eating, Bruno licks the bowl clean so it's ready for our next meal.

The whole family (even that Sofeeah) lays down on the couch together at night and watch this box with pictures on it. I like the pictures about food the best. Sometimes there are noisy pictures or this handsome guy that Lily calls Anderson Cooper. Funny name, huh?

Watching the Food Channel.

At the end of the day, Lily or Clive will say, "Go to sleep" and I know that means I go to my bed.

Every night I have good dreams of all the things and the people I love.

Junior is a Very Sweet Dog

Of Billy Fred, Jr., huMom June Cooper says, "Junior is a very sweet dog." Born and abandoned, then abused, Junior was six weeks old in 2005 when June and Billy became aware of his presence in an empty Villa Nova house.

Junior had one advocate; his Tia. She was an agile German Shepherd mix who came over the wall of June and Billy's house, got food, and took it back over the wall to Junior. She was not at all friendly, showing her teeth to June and Billy when they tried to pet her. Always, she kept her distance.

One day while Tia was away, June got the puppy and brought him home. He rolled up into Billy's arms and turned his soulful eyes upward. Billy melted and the fur ball became his namesake.

About three days after Junior had settled into his new home, Tia came over the wall again, shook paws with Billy, and lay down beside him. She was part of the family now, and no one ever saw Tia's teeth in anger again.

I love it when you cook for me in the morning!

Junior is afraid of the noisy highway and will not go anywhere in the car. However, he has, in the past, run under the car to hide from Tia, who was too big to go under it after him. It's hard to tell if Tia really was unable to get under the car, or if she just let Junior have his way. Tia could flatten herself well enough to get under the bed and sleep all night with her toys. It does seem she could have gotten under the car if she really wanted to.

In 2010, Tia crossed the Rainbow Bridge. Everyone in the family missed her, including Junior... at least for a few days. Tia played a special role in Junior's life, some of which he might never miss at all.

Even on his own, and without Tia's watchful eye and strict discipline, Junior remains a very sweet dog with whom Billy and June are happy to share their home and their lives.

Livin' the Good Life

My earliest memories are of living alone in a dark place where I felt scared all the time. I got adopted by a big dog in the neighborhood. She would leap over the wall and bring me food. Then she would leave and I would be scared again. She encouraged me to eat and rest and get big and strong. Then, she said, she would teach me how to get by in the world outside. I had my doubts about that. I thought of her as my aunt, so I called her Tia.

One day this lady came and gathered me up from my dark place where I was hiding. My Tia wasn't around, so I was shaking. What if she couldn't find me again? What if somebody hurts me?

The lady took me to a pretty place and gave me to a big man. He was so warm that when I rolled into his arms, I felt really secure for the first time in my life. I stopped shaking. I was in a safe place.

Next thing I knew, my Tia was back! I was so happy to see her. She moved in and started taking care of me full time. Sometimes I would do something that my huMom didn't want me to do, and Tia would explain to me what was expected of me. If I got stubborn about it, Tia would really explain to me what was expected of me.

One day a while back, I noticed Tia was gone. I guess I had finally learned everything I needed to know. She probably went off to find another puppy to raise. I'm a testament to how good she was at that. I'm very self-disciplined, and I owe it all to Tia.

For example, I'm up every morning at the crack of 8:00. I don't bother anybody for food until time for the mid-day meal. Then I have a nice comida around two in the afternoon. Then I eat again before bed. The only thing that breaks my routine is June cooking dog food at 6:00 a.m. I can't sleep through that. Gotta eat!

I learned from Tia how to train Billy. I like to sit on the back of my recliner and look out the window, especially now that Tia is gone. I need to know what's going on outside. Sometimes I find Billy sitting in my chair. I have to give him "the look" until he gets the message and moves.

Get off the chair, Billy.

I won't be leaving Billy the way Tia left me. Even after all these years, I still have to remind him about the recliner. HuMom would have such a hard time if I wasn't here to keep him in line. Besides, I'd miss her yummy homemade food. They both need me and, well, I need them, too.

Beauty and the Not So Beastly Beast

A neighbor of Angela's in Maine had two small kids and wanted a dog to make the family complete. She headed for the local shelter in search of a cute little white dog. She came home with an Australian Cattle Dog-Lab mix. He was cute, just not small and fluffy. He was full of life and energy. She named the new dog Kryptonite because she had always loved Superman. The problem was, the kids did not think he was super and he wasn't actually in love with them either. Family life and toddlers were just not his style. Everyone was unhappy.

So Angela did the neighborly thing … she re-rescued him. He was rather traumatized, unruly and detached. What had she gotten herself into?

First, she shortened his name to Krypto. She spent a lot of time with him … bonding, training and rebuilding his confidence. With a name like Krypto he could not be a skittish weakling, afraid of his own shadow.

While he still looks tougher than he really is, Krypto is a lover, not a biter. And he loves to snuggle with Angela. He also loves to run. They lived on a hill at the ocean and Krypto became the leader of the beach bunch. Always first into the water, he was not above grabbing anyone's … or everyone's toys and taking them back to the beach

From age 16, Angela had wanted to live in Mexico. In 2011, she packed up her life, and Krypto, and moved to Lakeside. It was a dream come true for both of them. As much as Krypto loved the cold and snow of Maine, he relishes the heat of the sun in Mexico.

He was spending a lot of time just lying in the sun. Angela began to wonder if Krypto might need a playmate and with so many dogs looking for homes, the search began. One day, she saw an ad in Riberas del Pilar for a PLT (Poodle-Like-Thing), 15 pounds, mostly curls. This dog had been saved from abuse by two older and larger male dogs. She had been living on the street for quite a while and those white curls became grey, matted and infested. She had to be shaved down to her little pink body.

Angela knew she could help this little waif reach her potential. It had worked with Krypto. Hmmm, Krypto, how would he react? Just like a superhero, he licked her soft pink skin, was gentle with her and helped Angela nurture her back to robust health.

With her hair re-grown, fluffy and curly as nature intended, she prances when she walks contentedly beside Krypto. Angela has named her Prada and she has proudly grown into her name.

What *have* we gotten ourselves into ?

His Story

Ya want a story? OK, I'll tell ya a story…

It all started in this very pretty place with lots of water and rocks and trees. I ain't gonna tell ya about this family I lived with… that was just one big mistake. I have this need to herd stuff and they had these little people that, well were not cooperatin'… and that brought out the worst in me and the worst in the big humans as well… and I just didn't like livin' in a family… 'nuff said.

So this lady, Angela, she takes me to her house. We used ta walk on a beach and I had a gang of other dogs who followed me. I'd show them how ta act tough, even if they didn't look or feel it. It's like all about da image, ya know. My name is Krypto and I gotta live up to da image that implies. Yeah, I'm tough on da outside, more refined and gentle on da inside.

I'm livin' with Angela and we're gettin' along great. She's teachin' me stuff and I'm gettin' lotsa treats 'cause I'm learnin' fast. Like this…she calls my name. I come. I get a treat. You betta believe I'm comin' every time she calls just in case I get a treat.

I played outside a lot. Sometimes it got real cold and these little white things would slowly fall down from the sky. I'd run around tryin' to catch them in my mouth. I couldn't catch all of 'em so some of 'em would lie on the ground and make it all smooth and soft… and cold! I could do this for hours it was so much fun. Well, until my paws got cold. Angela, she just looked out the window and laughed.

One day we got in the car and drove for a long time. I'm bein' quiet and calm, just like Angela taught me. When we stop we're in a place that's very warm, with lotsa sunshine. Oooooooh, turns out I just looooooooooove to sleep in da sun. When I get too hot, I just find a nice shady spot on some cool tiles to continue sleeping.

Well one day, Angela, she brings home dis scrawny pink thing with no hair. I was wonderin' what da heck it was until I sniffed it. No problems, it was a pathetic little girl dog. I licked her and she cuddled up to me so I guess she liked it. She's so small and she needs someone like me to protect her. And I am a tough guy so I do. Angela calls her Prada... I think 'cause it means special.

What do you *think* I'm thinkin' ?

When we all go for a walk, Prada and I keep up da same pace. Angela says we look like "two peas in a pod"... you know what dat means, right? We sleep beside each other. She don't know much about toys. She just likes to chew on a cork from a bottle. Sometimes she teases me... she'll chew on me and bark at me and I'll pretend to get up and chase her. Just our little game, ya know?

She's learnin' to be real tough... sometime I think she's learning too well. She will go at big dogs, barkin' her head off. I gotta get in between and shoo her off. She just don't understand she's little.

I like livin' with my two ladies… I can be tough when I need to be and soft when I want to be.

The Beauty

rada: founded in 1913 in Milan, Italy, by Mario and Martino Prada... an Italian fashion label, specializing in luxury goods for men and woman. Well, that's how some people define it.

I *am* a Prada... a cute, curly white-haired PLT (that's a PRADA-Like-Thing to you) found on the street in 2012. I specialize in loving my huMom, Angela, and my bestie, Krypto.

While I've never been to Milan, Italy... I think it's just down the road from Chapala, or maybe the other direction... past Jocotepec... on the way to Guadalajara... oh, well, it doesn't really matter. It's farther than I ever want to go.

Like that other Prada, I started small... just a puppy... and not very fashionable. I lost my mom and was wandering around for a long time looking for her when these two, big, mean dogs came up to me. Oh, they were talking sweet things about me and being nice and then one started touching me in a place that I didn't like... down there, you know? So I was kind of crying 'cause I was scared and I didn't know what to do. A lady must have heard me because she came and grabbed me and took me away from those mean guys.

She looked at me and said, "You, my dear, are a mess!" Well I know my hair was kinda messy, and it needed a good wash 'cause it was all sticking together. And I was itchy because I think I had some bugs living on me. I might have smelled a bit too.

So she took me to a place where a man just looked at me, shook his head, and then got this loud machine that he put on my back. It kinda tickled as he moved it all over me. I closed my eyes because it felt nice. When the noise stopped, I opened my eyes and was shocked to see all my hair lying around me... and I felt a little chilly. Then they sat me in a tub and poured some stuff on me and rubbed me and then wrapped me in a towel that felt so warm. Next thing I know I'm in a box, with my towel, all alone. It

144

had been a pretty exciting evening so I just lay down and slept.

Yes, I *am* a Prada.

Now, I never did find my mom. I got a HuMom instead. Her name is Angela. I live with her and Krypto. He's the man of the house, pretty tough and real smart. He's also my best friend. He takes care of me and Angela. I'm always so proud to go out with them, I do this kinda skip-it-y-hop and sometimes, I stretch my neck and walk real straight, looking around. Angela says I'm prancing when I do that.

I loooooooooooooove humans. Whenever I can I'll jump on a lap and nuzzle into a human neck with my nose just behind an ear. Most humans smell soooooooo good. I usually get a rub on the back when I do this, so I kiss the neck and well, it just keeps going until… well… it stops.

When I'm tired, which is every night after a day with Krypto, we both like to lie on the sofa on either side of Angela. We'll be on our backs, legs in the air, and she just knows exactly what feels good. She's the best tummy-rubbing huMom in the world. Sometimes she stops too soon so I just bump her hand with my nose to remind her I'm not done enjoying myself yet.

Yeah, I'll probably never get to Milan to meet those other Pradas… I'm too happy where I am.

They Are Her Kids

Tere Ruiz has a beautiful and accomplished daughter, Andrea. While she wanted more children… six, she says!… that was not meant to be. When Andrea moved out on her own, Tere adopted dogs to fill her house and be her "kids."

When Andrea went from Mexico City to Ocotlan to start her business, Tere was sad and lonely. Andrea was desperately missing her Mom as well. One night, she came home from working and saw a puppy in front of her house. Being her mother's daughter, she took it inside. Perhaps this dog would keep her company. She called her Gorda, because the puppy was soooooo sweet. While Andrea was working, Gorda was misbehaving. She called her mom for help. Tere moved from Mexico City to Ixtlahuacan, a town about 2 hours from Ocotlan, and took over the raising of the puppy.

Gorda loves her siblings, Kilo and Lorenza. She plays with Kilo… and Lorenza is her partner in crime when it comes to rolling in disgusting smelly things… like cow poop. She watches Tere's every move. Gorda demands attention. She will jump on anyone's lap, put her paws on the person's shoulders and stare into their eyes. Given a smile or any bit of encouragement, she will then cover the person's face with kisses. She is the eldest of the kids.

During the rainy season of 2008, Lorenza came into Tere's life. She was taking her daughter to the bus stop. There was a large crowd of people. As they boarded the bus, a tiny little object, resembling a drowned rat, was left behind. As Andrea got on the bus, she begged her mom to take the poor thing home. Lorenza was the name Tere had picked out for her second child… so she decided that would be the name of her second puppy.

Like a hyperactive child, Lorenza's excess energy is due to her thyroid working overtime. When she is supposed to take her medicine she is hard to find… and harder to capture! When she wants Tere's attention she dances around and stands on her hind legs with her paws on Tere's waist. She licks Tere gently until the kisses are returned.

Lorenza is the scorpion hunter and protector of the house.

Tere and her family.

One night, when leaving her boyfriend Gerry's house, Tere noticed a tiny little dog on the street. He spotted her and ran under a car. She asked Gerry for a piece of chicken left over from dinner. She used it as bait to lure the little bit of a thing out from under the car. She picked it up and discovered it was a boy. She only wants female dogs so she generously handed the dog to her host. Based on his size, he was named Kilo.

Not long after, Tere moved in with Gerry and Kilo remembered her. He became Tere's bebé and she carried him around because he was so small. When she picked him up, he fell into her chest… just like an infant. He loves to cuddle… with anyone. His sweetness affects everyone… even the very tough looking handyman. Kilo has epilepsy, which does not hinder him from being a daring escape artist… or pursuing any exciting adventure. As the man of the house, he makes sure everyone is protected from strange noises and intruders.

Like any other family, they each have individual personalities and all have a lot of love.

Happy to Be Here

My name's Gorda. My first huMom named me that because I'm soooooo sweet. Blonde and sweet. She was named Andrea. She took me into her house and fed me. Then she went away for a long time. That was good, I could investigate things. And play with everything. When she came home she wasn't happy. She yelled at me for making a mess… with the stuff I played with… and when I peed and pooped. Well, I was just a baby and I didn't know what else to do. She loved me and fed me… she just didn't have time to teach me things.

One day her huMom, Tere, came and took me away to another house. Things were very different. I had to remember to go outside to pee and poop. I couldn't pull things out of drawers and baskets. I had real toys to play with… and sisters too. They were from Mexico City and kind of cool and aloof. They called themselves elegant and dignified. I called them snobs. I didn't mourn them very much when they crossed the Rainbow Bridge. In this new house, it was a little bit strange for a while. Then I got accustomed to what I could and couldn't do and I learned how to be a good dog.

Tere really loves me. She talks to me with her sweet voice. She holds me close and I like to snuggle with my nose in her breasts like I did with my mom. I like to watch her… and I know how to get her attention for a pat or a hug. When she's typing, I sit beside her and look at her until I get her attention. She smiles and says, "In a minute, Gorda" and of course, I don't know what a minute is, so I push her hand with my nose. That makes her laugh and sometimes she even stops typing.

I don't play with the other dogs very much. Sometimes I sneak out with Kilo. Usually, I just like to be around Tere… and Andrea. I love it when she comes to visit and sleep over. I sleep with her.

She was my first huMom and will always be very special to me. I'm very grateful that she took me into her house and was the first one to love me.

Occasionally, I get into trouble. It's because I can't resist tomatoes. They smell delicious. They taste so sweet. They're soft and they kind of explode in my mouth. If Tere puts a bowl of tomatoes on the table I know how to reach them. I jump on a chair, then onto the table. I'll sit there and just gobble them all up until Tere discovers me. She tells me I'm a bad dog and I don't mind because I love my tomatoes… and any other food I can get to, really.

You got me tomatoes … my favorite!

My favorite time is at night, when we're all in bed with Tere. Before we go to sleep she sings to us. She has a special song for each of us. Her voice is sweet and clear and lovely. When I hear my song, I just snuggle closer and smile. And I think how happy I am in this family.

Life Is Happy… and Sad

I remember being cold and wet. There were lots of people around me and no one seemed to notice me or hear me whimpering. I just wanted to convince someone to pick me up. When I'm dry I'm pretty… my hair is soft… I have beautiful green eyes… and a curly tail. No one could hear my pleas. I was very sad.

Suddenly all the people disappeared. I started to slowly walk away to look for some shelter. A lady came to me and picked me up. "Pobrecita," she said. And I started kissing her face. She laughed and she wrapped me in a blanket and took me to her home. She smiled at me a lot and called me Lorenza. I think that's a beautiful name. It makes me so happy to hear Tere call my name.

At her house there were already three dogs… two that were from Mexico City and wanted nothing to do with a waif like me. And one named Gorda. She's my big sister. We have matching chairs that we curl up in. She shows me how to be a good dog. Now we have Kilo… he's our brother. He's very cute and very funny.

When Gala, one of the Mexico City dogs, crossed over the Rainbow Bridge I cried. She lay down under the dining room table and went to sleep. She just never woke up. I lay down beside her for a while. I licked her and sniffed her. We didn't like each other much. Still I was sad to see her go.

I'm the watchdog for the house. I'm always roaming around watching what's going on. I need to keep moving. I've got so much energy, it's hard to slow down or stop. Just moving, moving, moving… sniffing under and around trees and bushes… checking on things… looking at everything… listening for strange noises. Those scorpions are the worst. They can really hurt dogs and humans. Whenever I see one I bark, good and loud. I even have different barks to let everyone know how big and dangerous the scorpion is. I'm happy to know I look out for everyone's safety.

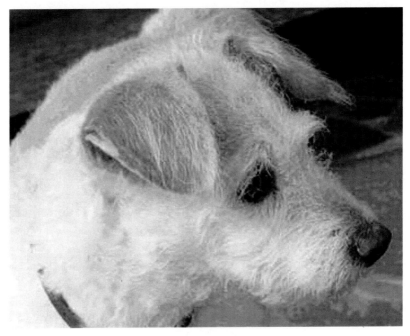

Thinking about my life... I'm happy.

It was so great to come and live at Gerry's house. I liked him a lot. He would play with us and walk with us. Then he got very sick. He would stay in bed a lot. I'd lie right beside him to try and make him feel better. Just like Gala, one day he stopped breathing. Me and Gorda and Kilo and Tere and Andrea, we all just lay on the bed next to him. Tere and Andrea talked to him and sang to him. We sniffed him and licked him and stayed close to him. That was a very sad day.

Now we all try to make Tere happy. I can stand on my hind legs and put my front paws on her waist. It's like we're dancing. I'll kiss her face, very gently. She'll laugh and kiss me right back. Sometimes she picks me up and my curly tail can wind around her wrist like a bracelet. She smiles and for that moment I know she's happy.

My life here is full. I have people and dogs that love me and I love them. I think we have to experience sadness so we can really appreciate our happiness, don't you?

Small Is Good

Are you aware of all the terms humans use for "smallish in stature?" Here's just a few of my least favorite… and in alphabetical order, I might add… diminutive, miniature, petite, pint-sized, puny, runt, teensy, undersized, wee. Quite frankly, I find all of them quite offensive and I'd like to remind you…and the world… that good things come in small packages.

My name is Kilo… guess why. I'm the man of the family. The only man in the house, which is tricky sometimes. I can't be letting any other male dogs near my sisters because you never know what they might try. I'm a guy so I have a pretty good idea. And there's absolutely no way I can let them near my hu-Mom, Tere.

She really understands me and calls me her baby. Maybe because I'm small… mostly because I'm the youngest. When I'm with her I can completely relax, because I know she'll protect me. And I love it when she holds me like a human baby. I feel so safe.

To tell you the truth, I do prefer to snuggle and be sweet… with everyone. Growling and barking and fighting just takes a lot of energy. And really, where… or what… does it get you? Yeah, I'm a cuddler. I just don't let too many people know. It would be bad for my reputation… so, keep it to yourself, OK?

I worry a lot because I have a disease called epilepsy. Oh sure, I take medicine for it… in my milk in the morning and at night. Sometimes when I get excited about something or run around too much, I have a seizure. My body shakes and freezes and I can't stop it and then when it's over I'm just really tired.

I'm pretty careful most of the time so I don't get over excited.

Small is the *best* when Tere holds me.

Like one time when I found this little critter in the yard… it was probably twice my size (most creatures are) and it seemed to be sleeping. I knew I should chase it off. I also knew I couldn't chase it too hard. So I poked it with my nose and rolled it around some. It seemed to be dead. I didn't kill it. It was already like this. I promise. I was scared I'd be in trouble for making it dead.

Well, Tere saw me and said. "Kilo, what are you doing?"... except she said it in Spanish because that's the language she uses sometimes. Anyway, she came over and started laughing. She told me it wasn't really dead... it was a 'possum and it was pretending to be dead. Whew, that was a close one.

Tere makes me stay in the house a lot. Sometimes, though, I just want to be free. I can usually find a way out to the street if I really want to. I'm clever at squeezing under and through things like gates and fences. That's one time my size is an advantage. I just like to get out, look around and hang out with some old street buddies. We wrestle and roll around and I end up getting itchy... those street guys have fleas.

One of my favorite things to do is to sit on the terrace at night and just look at the stars. They're tiny too. When you think about it, we're all pretty small in the universe, right?

There Once Was a Woman Who Lived In a Shoe

While living in her Oregon home, RoseAnn Wagner had always been a one dog person. That changed after she and her three cats moved to San Juan Cosala in September 1998. At that particular time, she didn't even have one dog.

RoseAnn met Lucy, a black and tan puppy, at the Lakeside Chili Cook-Off on Valentine's Day in 1999. It was love at first sight. Lucy accompanied RoseAnn to her home in the Racquet Club, where she integrated peacefully with the three cats. For the next six years, Lucy was the only dog. And RoseAnn's sensitivity to the plight of homeless dogs in Lakeside increased.

While walking with Lucy during an especially abundant rainy season in 2006, RoseAnn found flooding over the Jocotepec malecon and into the park. As she surveyed this somewhat unusual sight, she saw a little black thing bobbing in the water. On closer observation, she could see it was a puppy...swimming for its life. She enlisted the help of a passing stranger who waded in and got it.

The little dog appeared to have been a nursing mother. There were no puppies in sight. She was exhausted and emaciated. RoseAnn thought she looked like a concentration camp survivor and named her CC...or CiCi as it is now.

Cici was timid at first. She seemed to have the residual effects of a back leg injury, hopping around in favor of her left hind leg for about a year. Even so, she made friends with Lucy and the cats, settling herself in quite comfortably.

RoseAnn had moved from the Racquet Club into a large mountain side property in San Juan Cosala. Always an early riser, one morning in January of 2011, she opened the door into the

155

pre-dawn darkness to let everyone outside. Lucy and CiCi were quite excited with a find in their yard. RoseAnn got a flashlight to investigate.

RoseAnn's constant source of joy and good company.

An unfamiliar Rubbermaid tub had been placed on the ground inside the walls during the night. In it were two female black Lab mix puppies, each about the size of a drinking glass. The identical twins were squirmy and squealing for food. RoseAnn brought them inside where Rhoda and Mary, as close as the two characters from a favorite TV sitcom, soon became members of her expanding household. In addition to Lucy, CiCi, and the three cats, two more cats had joined the family in recent years.

It was July 4, 2012. RoseAnn was out walking with Rhoda and Mary when she spotted a small black puppy covered with mange, crouched in a corner. She collected him and took him immediately to the vet. While the dog was there, the gardener built a separate play area at the end of the property to keep the rest of the animals healthy. Despite best efforts, everybody got mange, including RoseAnn.

Of her newest addition, RoseAnn says, "He's lucky to be alive.

It's the reason his name is Lucky."

The dogs are a constant source of joy and good company. They have all found mutual peaceful co-existence, playing together on their expansive property and beginning each day with a good long walk through the mountainside or along the San Juan Cosala malecon.

Still sensitive to and saddened by the plight of the Mexican street dogs, RoseAnn says, "I could easily become one of those old women who lives in a shoe."

View from the Top

'mon in. Have a seat here on the sofa beside me, if you like. My name's Lucy and I'm the grande dame here on the Wagner Estate. Have been for almost 100 years. That'd be 14 years on your calendar. I can tell you anything you want to know about our canine crew. Feline, too, if you really want to know about them.

It all started at the Chili Cook-Off back in 1999. Valentine's Day. I'll never forget it. I was there with some other dogs who needed forever homes, too. I was an orphan then. RoseAnn looked at me. I looked at her. It was love at first sight. I went home with her that day. We've been together ever since.

In those years, we lived in a different place, less land, houses closer together. I started right in announcing people who were coming to see her. I was really small in those days and could slip through the design in the door and right out to the front gate. She loved it. People didn't even have to ring the doorbell.

When I moved in, there were three cats. More of them than me, and I was small. They let me know what was expected of me and I fit right in with them. I also did whatever RoseAnn wanted me to do. I loved her so much even then and I wanted to please her so I could always be with her. She didn't have to give me a command more than once, I'll tell you that.

Eventually, RoseAnn and I moved to the estate where we are now. More space, more room to run. I love it. It was during our first rainy season here that we found CiCi. That poor little girl… so pathetic, bobbing along in the water, sputtering, trying to swim.

She was so shy when she got here, I got right on making her feel comfortable.

CiCi and I had some good long talks. She'd lost all her babies in that flood where we found her. She was shaking as much for them as she was for herself. She said it was the worst day of her life. Worse even than the time she got hit on her hindquarter by a car. That took a long time to heal. She was hopping for a long time even after she got here.

I'm the Grande Dame here on the Wagner Estate.

CiCi'd had a hard life for a young dog… barely a year on your calendar. She thought she'd crossed the Rainbow Bridge and gone to heaven when RoseAnn brought her home. I showed her the ropes, showed her how to make peace with the cats, told her I'd always be here for her…that she had a home now. The best home she could imagine, from my viewpoint. She respected that and has been a good dog ever since.

CiCi and I headed out into the darkness early one morning, as we always do. As I said, we have a lot of land to run and patrol, and we take care of business out there as well. We always looked forward to those early mornings outdoors. This particular morning, there was something strange in the yard. We approached it with caution.

It was a box made out of something you couldn't really tear with your teeth. There was no lid on it. CiCi and I looked inside. There were two tiny black puppies wriggling and squealing all over the place. I knew right away that I had my work cut out for me, and by this time, I'm along in years.

As I predicted she would, RoseAnn brought the puppies inside and started fattening them up and helping them grow. And did they grow! And grow! They're identical twins. RoseAnn calls them Rhoda and Mary. I brought them along just as I had CiCi.

We had a couple more cats by then. Two cats… ten cats, doesn't make much difference. They keep to themselves and don't bother with anybody unless you get in their faces. Even then, once they know you they just go to sleep or walk away. So I taught the twins about the cats and about everything else they needed to know to have the good life here.

Over time, Rhoda started to show promise as a leader. She's especially bright and sensitive to the energy in our house and to what's going on with the other dogs… and the cats. As I said, I'm getting along in years. I owe it to RoseAnn to make sure she's cared for by everyone who lives here. I want her never to have to worry about any of the dogs. And, just between us, I know after I'm gone she'll find a stray who needs a home and give it one. So I want someone in place who can train the new dog. I've groomed Rhoda for all of that and she's eased right into it.

Now this last one I have to tell you about really brought some craziness when he came. Rhoda and Mary were with RoseAnn when she found him. He had these little critters all in and under his skin. Tiny little things you can't even see and they eat your skin and make your hair fall out. That dog was a mess!

And on closer examination, he was almost dead. All of us got whatever he had. Even RoseAnn. Personally, I don't ever recall being so uncomfortable. It didn't last long and the next thing I knew, RoseAnn was calling him Lucky. Good name. He was lucky I didn't throw his mangy carcass out of here, especially when I got what he had myself.

The thing is, I have an image to uphold here. I can't be coming this close to the end of my life and getting short tempered with sickly pups. Lucky turned out to be a really fun addition to our home. He's closer in age to Rhoda and Mary and they love having somebody to play and run with them.

Their favorite game is the three of them grab the same stick and hold onto it. "Three dogs on a limb," I call them when they do that. RoseAnn went away for a while. When she came back she brought treats and toys for all of us. The thing she got for Lucky and the twins is a ball with four big rope-like loops on it so they can all hold onto it at the same time without falling over each other.

I need to excuse you now. Rhoda wants my attention. She has a question about something. I command from the couch here. I'm sure you understand. Thanks so much for stopping by. I enjoyed telling you about our family. I love them. All of them. Even the cats. And especially RoseAnn.

Frequent Flyers

Once upon a time, a hairdresser in New Jersey decided to hang up the scissors and blow dryer and explore the world. Kathleen Morris found it easy to become a world traveler and adventurer. She enjoyed taking the roads less traveled and learning about different cultures. Each place broadened her horizons and brought her new friends.

In 1993, while in a small drinking establishment in Guatemala, she struck up a conversation with an Australian gentleman called Lindsay. She bought him a beer and according to a legend (no one remembers quite which one), they became friends for life. He would visit her in the United States and they would go on an adventure. A couple of years later, she went to Australia and they hit the road to all parts of that country. And their traveling sagas continue.

Kathleen moved to Lakeside in 1997. In 2000, Lindsay was visiting. One Saturday, they were sightseeing in Guadalajara, near the Libertad Market, when she spotted a puppy on the street. It had a very pretty looking coat with a double layer of hair that was dry and soft. It had no collar, no tags and did not seem to be with anyone. The dog was friendly and seemed in good shape. Kathleen decided to give it a home.

Her intention was to take it to the shelter on Monday. They all returned to Riberas for dinner and then a walk. By the time they returned to the house, the dog was heeling like a dog show champion. Lindsay commented, "She's gonna be a good dog for someone." Sunday, there were another couple of walks and some playing in the yard with the puppy. Monday morning, Kathleen took it for another walk. On her return, Lindsay said, "If you're gonna keep her, you're gonna have to call her Aussie." And she did.

Their bags are packed... ready to go!

Aussie's lineage is unknown... Kathleen lovingly describes her as a real "Heinz 57"... she most resembles a herding type dog, black and tan, with a white face and very deep and soft brown eyes. Kathleen discovered Aussie's love for kittens when she rescued one. She had it wrapped in a towel where Aussie could not see it. Aussie was circling around Kathleen, sniffing and jumping, trying to see what was in the towel. When she put it on the floor, Aussie stood protectively over the kitten. Mac the Cat adores her Aussie and they are great friends.

Around 2009, Kathleen decided to build a house near a beach. Once it was completed, she became a foster huMom with ALMA Humanitaria A.C., the humane society of Los Barriles in Baja California Sud and surrounding areas. Here's what Kathleen says about her role at ALMA: "While I am fostering I feel it is my job to not just to feed and love them... to train them with a few simple commands that will make them more adoptable and so their life will be much easier in the new home."

Every six months, Kathleen, Aussie and Mac the Cat fly to Baja for a few months.

Scruffy, whose name describes the coarse hair of her coat, came into their lives in 2012 when Kathleen saw a little puppy chained to a fence with no food, no water and surrounded by a lot of dried poop. She had been there a while. Kathleen bent down, talked softly to her and got the cable wire off of the pup's neck. When they got home, the first order of business was a bath.

The next day, Kathleen put the word out that she had a cute little dog, probably about six months old, of undetermined breed, who needed adopting. In the meantime, she began training Scruffy to make her more adoptable. Scruffy is a lover. She quickly wormed her way into Kathleen's heart as well as the hearts of Aussie and Mac the Cat.

Now there's another frequent flyer in the family.

The Star of the Show

So, I'm sniffin' around the market like I always do. As usual there's lotsa people walkin' around. Some bump into me like they don't see me. Sometimes they yell at me when that happens. Like it's my fault?

Well, this human comes over and starts talkin' to me... real nice and soft and gentle. She pats me on the head, and scratches behind my ears... my weak spot. She picks me up and holds me real close. And she takes me to her house. We were in a car for a long time to get there and it was worth the trip. She's got a real pretty place with a garden. She feeds me and then we go for a walk.

While we're walkin' she's talkin' to me. The other human doesn't say much. Sometimes if I walk too fast and get in front of her she pulls on the leash, gently, and I slow down. Same thing if I try to walk away or even run away. So, I get it, when we go away from the house and I'm on a leash, I just stay close to her side. That seems simple enough. Kathleen is my huMom and she teaches me a lot of stuff about how to be a good dog.

Now here's a story that might surprise you... I was in a play. Yup, little old Aussie is an actor!

I had to audition against another dog and I won. I think it's because Kathleen has taught me so much about how to listen to her and do what she says. Anyway, me and Kathleen played almost ourselves... I mean she was a human and I was a dog. When I came on stage people would laugh and clap and say "awwwwww." Humans say that a lot when they like dogs.

At the end of the show the curtain closed. Then it opened again and we all went to the edge of the stage. The humans were holding hands and bending over and I thought they were lookin' for something so I walked off the stage and was looking in front of the people, sniffin' and lookin' under their chairs.

People were laughin' and pattin' me and tellin' me I did a good job. I never did find anything so I looked up at Kathleen. She gave me a signal and I ran right back to her and sat beside her like I'm supposed to. And she scratched my ears (oooooooo, in my weak spot) and told me I was a good dog.

No autographs … please.

Oh, yeah… and here's another funny story. Humans think it's weird about me and Mac the Cat. I just love that little guy! And I have since the first day Kathleen brought him home. I knew she had a surprise for me. It was all wrapped up in a blanket and making these sad little mew-y noises. I wanted to see it so I was runnin' circles around Kathleen and jumpin' up, tryin' to see. Finally, Kathleen puts the towel down and carefully opens it and there lies the cutest little thing I have ever seen! I started to lick it, real gently because it was soooooooooooo tiny and soooooooooooo soft. It got up on its teeny, tiny legs and started to walk towards the door. "Uh-oh," I thought. It's too little to go out on its own. So I'm walking around it, tryin' to herd it back to the blanket. It moved pretty fast so I was runnin' in circles... I musta looked silly. Anyway, finally I had to pick it up in my teeth, very carefully, by its neck. I walked back to the blanket. I put my paws in front of me on the floor and verrrry softly put the kitten down and it just lay there, between my paws. We both sighed.

Kathleen brings a lotta dogs home. They don't stay very long. She teaches them stuff and they go to another house. I help her. My job is to give them some guidance, if you know what I mean. Any of them who don't respect her or Mac the Cat hears from me. I'm like "The Enforcer." Hmmmm, maybe I could make a movie one day.

Scruffy

My neck hurts. My throat's sore. My tummy's making sounds. I'm tired. I want to get away from this place because it smells of pee and poop. I know I don't smell very nice. I can't help it. I've been here for a long time. Humans walk by. I try to jump up and wag my tail to get their attention. Some of them look at me, most of them don't. Well, it's getting dark; I think I'll lie down for the night.

I was almost asleep when I heard a gentle voice talking. I opened my eyes and a human was almost lying down with me and talking to me... to me! So I sat up and wagged my tail and she got the thing off my neck that was making it hurt.

She took me to her house and gave me a bowl of water that I drank so fast I almost drowned. Oh, my throat was starting to feel soooooo much better. My neck still hurt because the thing that was around it had rubbed off all my hair. She gave me something to eat, which I gobbled down as fast as I could so my tummy would stop making noises. Then she put me in the sink and washed me with nice warm water and lots of bubbles. I smelled sooooo good.

I felt good too. The human sat down and I jumped on her lap and lay against her like I've seen baby humans do. She looked and at me and talked to me very quietly. I looked at her and I wanted to lick her face right off because she was being so nice to me. I think I fell asleep that way.

The next day, she gave me more water and food. The human said to me, "I am Kathleen... and this is Aussie," and she pointed to a big old dog lying on the floor, "and that's Mac the Cat," and she looked over at a cat asleep on the couch. Huh. I guess they live here too. Then she said, "I think I'm going to call you Scruffy because of that hair of yours."

So, now that I knew who everyone was, I was looking for

something to do. I found a basket with some toys in it. So I picked one up and took it over to Aussie. I shook it at him. I'm pretty sure I saw him smile. He tried to grab it. I kept it away from him and then he got it away from me. And I got it back. And we played like that until we both dropped down on the floor beside each other, panting. Aussie's a good old guy.

I just looooooove Baja.

Kathleen takes for me for walks… sometimes with Aussie and sometimes just her and me. She tells me stuff and teaches me things. I can shake hands, high five, roll over and play dead. Kathleen gives me treats when I do everything just the way she tells me.

Oh, wow… I see Kathleen putting stuff in a suitcase so I think we're all going on a trip again. Aussie, Mac the Cat and I love to go on trips with Kathleen. My favorite place is the beach… I hope we're going to Baja. I love it there!

Just the Two of Us...For a While

Stephanie Arnoldi and Barney migrated from Canada to Ajijic in 2007. "Just the two of us," Stephanie says. "No furniture. One chair. One TV. A blow-up bed." She and big, beautiful Barney with his long reddish hair and soulful eyes, began to create a home and a new life together in Villa Nova.

One day after household goods and furnishings had arrived, and the house looked more like a lived-in home, Stephanie went to Pemex to investigate the source of a gasoline leak in her car. While there she was befriended by a jovial little dog. Homeless, he had been hanging out around the gas station. He appeared to be mostly Dachshund so Stephanie named him Oscar Mayer. He was happy at home with Barney and Stephanie spoiling him. He could not have been more perfectly behaved in every way, and he seemed truly to believe he was an "only dog."

Everyone has a special place in her heart.

As Stephanie, Barney, and Oscar Mayer were walking through their neighborhood one day in 2009, they came upon the freshly groomed, beautiful Miniature Schnauzer who lived nearby. They walked with him toward his home only to discover a beautiful Miniature Schnauzer already in the yard there. So who was this little guy? Stephanie ran ads and talked among the dog-owner network for more than two weeks. No one responded. So Scooter-of-indeterminate-age joined the family. Stephanie describes him as "the perfect dog." Oscar Mayer was neutral. Barney just loved everybody.

In April 2010, another car issue, this time it was a tire, took Stephanie out to Riberas de Pilar near where the Animal Shelter dog kennels were located at the time. She saw a man walking a Medium Schnauzer. "Love your dog," she said. The man responded, "Not my dog. I'm just walking her."

Her name was Gracie. She was about six months old, fearful, and clearly accustomed to living on the streets. With Stephanie's training and guidance, she has grown into a gentle, gracious lady and the alpha dog in the house. Still, Oscar Mayer remained neutral, and Barney just loved her as he loved everybody.

In February of 2013, Stephanie's friend, Ian, found a little dog on the centerline of the highway. Ian was ill and Mickey, his one-eyed, one-year-old, fuzzy Chow mix, was all he could manage. The puppy needed a loving home. Ian called Stephanie for help finding one.

Stephanie went to Ian's house and scooped the tiny dog into her hand.

"She's ugly," Stephanie observed, and thought she might be a Chihuahua. Stephanie brought the little creature with the giant ears home to nurture while she found her a forever home. Yoda spent much of her early weeks in a canvas tote bag, away from Oscar Mayer who hated her. Barney, of course, continued to love everybody.

When Stephanie's friends, Patti and John, asked to "borrow" Oscar Mayer during their visit Lakeside, Stephanie obliged. They were so taken with him that they asked Stephanie if they could take him home for the summer. It was the second step toward

Oscar Mayer's forever home on another lakeside...in Ontario...where he truly is the "only dog" he thinks he is.

Meanwhile, Yoda turned out not to be a Chihuahua at all. She does behave like she thinks she is. At seven months, she weighed 50 pounds and was continuing to grow… although not into her ears which remain disproportionately large. Stephanie refers to her as "Baby Hughey" because she curls up in what she treats as the "corner" of a chair expecting Stephanie to sit beside her… on the four square inches that remain of the cushion surface. Stephanie has long since made the decision that her home is Yoda's forever home.

Barney crossed the Rainbow Bridge in April of 2013. Ian followed in July of the same year. Stephanie brought Ian's Mickey home to live with her, Scooter, Gracie, and Yoda. Now it is quiet, gentle Mickey who loves everybody.

Stephanie's Treasure

Hi. I'm Scooter. I wasn't always named Scooter. I used to be called Kasper. I had four brothers, and all our names started with the letter "K." I got separated from Karl, Keifer, Konrad and Klaus when we were just puppies.

I had a nice home growing up, with my own bed in the room where my human family spent most of their time. I had toys, too. Once in a while someone would even play with me.

One day, we went in the car. I loved to go in the car! So we went in the car to visit a girl dog who looked a lot like me. My folks talked with her folks and I visited with the girl dog, getting acquainted, letting her check me out. She was pretty cute and I kind of got lost in all that loveliness and getting acquainted and...well...we don't need to go into all that.

Later I went to get my folks from where I'd left them and they were gone! Did they forget me? Impossible! They were in trouble. I had to find them, so I took off. I looked for them in the day time and slept under the cover of bushes and shrubs at night.

The second day on my hunt, I ran into Barney and Oscar Mayer and asked them if they'd seen my folks. They said they had not and invited me to walk with them and their Stephanie. They said I could come home with them if we couldn't find my family. We didn't find my family.

When we got to their house, I ran inside and through this great room and out onto their patio and the next thing I knew I was in the water! Stephanie laughed and came toward me. Before she could get to me, I'd scooted myself right out of it.

"You're a strong little guy to get out of the pool all by yourself," she said to me. That's when she started calling me Scooter. Pool. I'd never seen a pool.

We've been together ever since that day. I never found my family and was happy to make a new home with Stephanie,

Barney, and Oscar Mayer. There were rules. Stephanie said I couldn't get on her bed, so I don't. When she's awake, I just lie on the floor and wait for her to doze off. Then I jump up and burrow under the covers beside her. She doesn't even know I'm there.

Wanna take a dip in the pool?

We've had some changes over the years since I came here. The most significant, I guess, is that I had what Stephanie calls "an operation." Now I don't go out with girls anymore. The hardest was watching Barney cross the Rainbow Bridge. The easiest was the disappearance of Oscar Mayer. Our family has grown. Even as it does, I know Stephanie treasures me. I hear her say so.

The Boss

My earliest memories are of cold, hard concrete. I slept on it. A lot. I was a baby and sometimes my Mom would come lay beside me so I could get some milk from her. Then one day she just stopped coming. I was on my own.

I wandered the streets looking for food and trying to find a safe place to stay. I learned from some of the older females that life on the street is dangerous for young girl dogs, so I laid low. Life was hard.

I got used to my neighborhood, learned where to find food and how to survive. At the same time, my neighborhood got used to me. After a while, some humans noticed I was homeless. I guess they thought they were doing me a favor by taking me to a place where I had to live in a cage. The food was regular, and really pretty good compared to what I'd been eating. Still, I missed my freedom and familiar places and faces.

What kept me from losing it in the cage place was that I got to go out every day. I made it really clear to the person who took me that I needed to leave. First he put a thing around my neck. Then he connected another long thing to it that he held onto. This combination made it really hard for me to get away. I was working on it when we ran into Stephanie out on the street.

When Stephanie and I made eye contact, I felt warm inside where my heart is. I knew I had to be with her...and be like her. I guess she felt it, too. At least she felt the part of wanting me with her. Pretty soon I was living in her house with three other dogs.

Yes, I'm in charge. Have a seat. I'll fill you in.

Stephanie spent a lot of time with me, teaching me manners, teaching me how to be a lady, and teaching me how to keep the others in line. Now I'm the boss around here. I'm gracious about it. Maybe that's why Stephanie calls me Gracie. Dogs come and dogs go, and they all know I'm in charge.

Ian's Legacy

'm Mickey. I'm 11 years old and I'm the new "old man" here in Stephanie's house. I've had a bit of a rough patch lately, so bear with me as I tell you what's going on. My energy's good. I'm very healthy. I just choke up a bit when I think about certain things.

These youngsters know how to keep an old man on is feet!

A long time ago when I was living on the street, I got into a terrible fight. I don't even remember what it was about. I know I didn't start it. On the street, you have to stand up for yourself in order to stay alive. I was pretty badly beaten up. I don't even know how I got to the hospital. I just remember waking up there and I couldn't see out of my right eye anymore. As I got better and was able to be outdoors running around, I couldn't run the same way either. I sort of bounce now on both front feet and then both back feet... like a kids' rocking horse.

Ian came for me in the hospital. I'd never seen him before. He just said he heard about me and he knew I'd need a safe place to be in the world. That was the beginning of a long and loving friendship. I loved Ian more than anything. We settled in to grow old together.

One day in February, Ian and I were out doing errands when he stopped the car on the side of the road. I watched him walk out to the center lane of the highway and scoop up this ugly little life form. I had no idea what it was. That was just like Ian... and that lump of life in the road could have been me a few years back.

You know, I may never grow into my ears.

Near as I could tell, it was a dog. More like a pair of giant ears with a dog attached. Ian called his friend, Stephanie. I heard him tell her he wasn't able to care for a puppy. He asked her if she'd keep the little creature until a home could be found for it. Soon Stephanie came to our house. "Yoda," she called it. I don't know what a Yoda is. She put it in a canvas tote bag and left.

I always thought because of my early life injuries that I'd cross the Rainbow Bridge before Ian did. I was wrong. As I lay beside Ian on his bed in July, I could feel the life slipping out of his body. I held close to him trying to coax it back, and he kept telling me that I would be all right. We stayed that way for two days. Then some people came.

I was alone again. Only now I was also old and blind in one eye.

I wasn't alone for long. Stephanie came and got me and took me to her house. The first thing I noticed when I got there was Yoda. How could I miss her? She's the biggest dog in the house! Even so, she still hasn't grown into her ears. Apparently Stephanie got attached to her and decided to keep her.

I wasn't here long when I figured out how Yoda got so big so fast. Stephanie makes our food. She mixes raw carrots with rice, chicken livers, and hearts and adds it to our kibble. Oh my! All of us, even an old guy like me, are full of energy.

Gracie (she's the boss around here) and I are very well-behaved on our walks. Yoda is still a puppy and needs to be reigned in. Scooter is a bit over-protective, so Stephanie keeps him close as well.

When Yoda and Scooter are here at home, they're funny to watch. They play together all the time. Scooter runs under Yoda and bites her leg. She falls down. Scooter laughs and runs away, with Yoda after him. Meanwhile, the regal Gracie sits on the back of the sofa and surveys our domain. What we all enjoy most is the way Stephanie laughs with us.

I miss Ian. He is in the place of un-forget in my heart that I can feel every time it beats. Even so, I feel very welcome as the new old man in Stephanie's home. Now it is my home, too.

Animal Lover

In 2009, Ken left England to find his place in the sun… and to meet a woman he had been corresponding with on the Internet. He landed in Guadalajara. In his hotel he met a fellow who told him about Manzanillo… a busy port city with lovely beaches located on the west coast of Mexico. He decided to go and check it out for a couple of days. While things did not work out, romantically, with his lady friend, Ken did fall in love with Manzanillo. He returned to England, sold all his worldly goods and returned to Manzanillo with two suitcases.

Ken found a comfortable place to live on the hill above the tourist zone. He enjoyed the sun and the surf of the Pacific Ocean and frequently walked along the shore. One day he came across a chocolate Lab. She had been living on the beach and trying to scrounge food, rather unsuccessfully, from the beach bars. She was pretty skinny and was infested with fleas and ticks. He fell in love with her huge liquidy brown eyes and took her home… via the veterinary office to get her shots. She cleaned up well and he called her Maya.

He began dog-sitting a friend's three-year-old Whippet named Yolanda. Over the three-year period that he and Maya looked after Yolanda, she delivered a litter of six puppies, was diagnosed with cancer, had radiation treatments and recovered.

Maya gained weight easily and was healthy. She ran around the verandah and in and out of the house. Ken would take his "girls" out walking three times a day. This activity caught on and soon he was walking several other dogs from the neighborhood. All of them loved the beach… except Maya. Surprisingly for a Lab, she does not like the water. She watches the tide and the other dogs play and is quite content to stay high and dry.

Ken and his favorite four legged ladies.

One evening, when Ken was strolling around Manzanillo, a friend who was a street vendor said, "I have a young lady I want you to meet." Ken was intrigued. The man then reached down and held up a scrawny cat he called Lady Gaga. She looked like she hadn't eaten in weeks. Ken took pity on her and took her home. It turns out she's actually Boy George and her… uh…his name was changed accordingly.

Maya accepted Boy George into the household very easily… almost too easily. She seemed to be slowing down and not running as much. Ken noticed her really struggling to get up one morning. He took her to the vet and she was diagnosed with hip dysplaysia. Ken has some hip problems too, and they are both on the same medication!

Things began to change in Manzanillo… the weather could be very oppressive in the summer months, the cost of living was increasing. On the Internet, Ken had reunited with an old friend from the RAF (Royal Air Force). This friend was living in the Chapala area. He spoke very highly of the people, the climate and the cost of living. So in May of 2012 Ken, Maya and Boy George moved to Lakeside.

Soon after, a friend of Ken's told him about a dog who had been abandoned at a construction site. It had been attacked by some other dogs and was taken to Lucky Dogs Animal Rescue. He went out to see her. He knew her as soon as he saw her... and she perked up when she saw him. She walked over, allowed him to pet her and they've been together ever since.

He calls her Sweetie, because it describes her nature so perfectly. She is kind and generous to everyone she meets whether they have two legs or four.

A Lot of Living

In dog years, I'm about 25. That doesn't sound old. I sure do feel old. I've roamed around. I've seen lots of things… some good… some not so good. I've met lots of people and dogs. Some of them were good to me and some were not. I've never stayed anywhere for a long time, I always seem to be on the move. I've done a lot of living.

For a while I lived on a beach and I liked rolling around on the sand. I'd roll a lot because I felt itchy and it seemed like a good way to scratch everywhere. Sometimes it got really hot… I'd see other mutts go in the water. I never did. It made a loud noise when it crashed on the sand and it moved in and out. Just didn't interest me. I'd rather look for some shade to cool off. Food was hard to come by, especially during the day. Sometimes I could find some at night. That was dangerous… people would always holler at me to go away. A few even chased me with brooms. Come on, I thought, a girl's gotta eat!

I met a real nice man on the beach. His name is Ken and he took me home. We made one stop for me to get some shots and a bath. That bath stopped my itching, so now I just roll around for fun. His house has this big porch that I like to lie on. I can go in and out of the house anytime I want. Ken feeds me… it's so nice not to have to scrounge around anymore.

I don't move very fast… my hips hurt when I do. Ken and I take pills in the morning. I think his hips hurt too. I move slowly and hop up and down stairs. I'm learning how to do stuff that's not painful.

Ken brought home a cat one night. He thought it was a girl and he called her Lady Gaga, which I thought was a silly name. Turns out the funny part is… the cat's a boy. Now he calls him Boy George. I don't know how he comes up with these names. Anyway, Boy George just does his thing and I do mine.

I *look* good for my age.

One day this cute little thing called Sweetie came to live with us. She's really kind and full of life and energy... like I wish I was. She had a tough time with Boy George at first. He hissed at her and swatted her a few times so now she just lets him be. She's one smart dog.

Ken takes us in the car sometimes. I like to lay in the back seat. Sweetie gets all excited and jumps around from the front to the back. Sometimes if my hips are really giving me pain, I'll stay in the car all afternoon. I just don't feel like moving. Ken will check on me, maybe bring me a treat or some water. He understands.

Sweetie is good company... she makes me laugh at the way she runs and jumps all over the place. She's curious about everything. Probably because she's just a kid... she's only about 7 in dog years... she's got a lot of living to do.

Sweetie

OK, I don't know where my mom went. I barely remember her. I've been on my own forever. I was in a place where some guys were building something and they would feed me from what they were eating and give me water. At night, I guess they went home to their moms and I would sleep… anywhere I wanted. Sometimes I slept under the stars. Mostly I slept inside the building.

Then the guys stopped coming and it was really lonely. And I didn't have any food or water. Where am I supposed to get that stuff? They didn't tell me. One night a pack of dogs found me. They seemed mad that I was sleeping. They started barking and biting me. I didn't know what I did wrong. I was scared. They were growling and one took a big bite out of my back leg. Owwww… that really hurt. They were pushing and shoving and nipping at me. I stopped fighting back. I was too tired and sore. I just lay down quietly. They stared at me and growled for a while and then they went away. Whew. Now what? I didn't know what to do… hungry, tired, in pain… maybe if I just lie here. I slept for a while and woke up. I didn't feel any better. I was too weak to look for food or water so I just went back to sleep.

What's that? I heard some footsteps. Were they friendly or frightening… I just didn't know. I lay still. They came closer. I opened one eye, just a little bit. Hey! It was one of my guys. He seemed surprised to see me. I wagged my tail. I tried to get up… my leg wouldn't hold me so I fell down again.

He came over and lifted me up. "Oh, pobrecita," he said. He took off his shirt and wrapped it around me. He took me to a place where a lot of dogs lived. They put me in a room with a wire door so I could see outside. Somebody washed me and fixed my leg so it didn't hurt so much. They wrapped something around it. I got lots of water to drink and some food. After a few days I could walk again. I even started running around with the other dogs.

A man came and looked at me one day. I looked right back at him. He walked around with me and I kept looking at him, hopefully. Then I showed him my trick… I can chase my tail! I think that's what did it. He started laughing… and I went home with him!

Whew… chasing my tail makes me thirsty!

He, well now we, have a pretty nice place. It has another dog, Maya. She's kind of old and has trouble moving fast. She's very gentle and she loves to watch me play. Then there's a very odd cat. He's so mean… I tried to play with him and make friends. No way! He hissed at me! And when I wanted to lick him, he smacked me! I'm staying away from him; he's no fun at all.

I feel bad for Maya because she hurts so much. I play as hard as I can and she enjoys watching me. When we go in the car, I get very excited and she calmly sits in the back seat. When I take a rest, I curl up in my special chair right next to the couch where she likes to lay down.

Sometimes Ken tries to go on an adventure without me. I'm always watching him so I know the signs. One time I jumped over the wall, squeezed under a fence and was waiting for him at the gate when he was driving out. I was pretty proud of myself and barked at him to let him know he forgot to take me. He got out of the car and put me in and we went to the golf course. He rode around on a cart all day and I got to sit right beside him. I sat up straight and I didn't bark. He told me I was his sweetie. He'd scratch my head. Lots of guys came and talked to me and petted me. They would shake their heads and laugh.

When I got home that night and told Maya, she smiled. She just loved that story.

Now You See Him. Now You Don't

Damyn Young and his partner, John Martin, had already been Lakeside for two years when they attended a Christmas party in 2005. Damyn recalls mixing and mingling with 150 or so guests in the Chula Vista Norte home of friends.

As the evening wore on, Damyn noticed that every time the hostess opened the door for a departing guest, a little black mutt with floppy ears covered in burrs would come in.

Guests noticed him, of course, and the attention caused him to roll over, put his feet up, and make himself available for a belly rub or some other gesture of affection. After this happened a couple of times, the hostess began asking guests if they wanted a dog. No one had had quite that much to drink.

As the crowd thinned, the hostess found Damyn on the terrace where he'd been most of the evening and asked if he wanted to take the dog home. "What dog," Damyn asked, feigning ignorance. "Oh, do come with me," was the answer.

Damyn picked up the dog, handed him to John who handed him back. They both knew their lifestyle would not work for a dog. They finally agreed to take him for the night and see if they could find either the owner or a home for him the next day.

I do love to party with John and Damyn!

The dog was a temporary house guest and Damyn and John wanted to call him something other than "dog"… something party-ish since they found him at a party. After rejecting a couple of possibilities, they settled on Tequila.

Tequila was very well behaved, looked well cared-for (except for the burrs in his ears) and was housebroken. It appeared to Damyn that Tequila had either wandered off or had been dumped. After a trip to the groomer the day after the party, Damon put up signs in Chula Vista Norte.

No one responded.

At the end of the first 24 hours, Tequila disappeared from Upper Chula Vista. John and Damyn couldn't find him anywhere. Of course, he didn't have tags yet. He wasn't their dog. This time the signs went up in Chula Vista.

One of the agents who worked at the real estate office at the bottom of the hill saw the signs. He called to say the secretary in his office had retrieved a little black dog from the traffic-laden carretera. She had decided to adopt him as the office dog when Damyn and John came in to rescue him…again… and not for the last time.

About a week later, when it was pitch black outside the house, Tequila disappeared again. He jumped over a wall on the back of the property and got tangled in a huge hedge where he had gone exploring. They found him not because he was barking. He wasn't. They found him because they could hear the hedge rustling as he wagged his tail.

Three days later, he did it again. This time he had tags and Damyn received a call within 24 hours. He had made his way off the mountain and down into San Antonio Tlayacapan. A couple of young boys decided he would be a fun addition to their family. Their mother thought otherwise and made them return Tequila to his rightful home.

This time added precautions were in order. Damyn tied Tequila on a length of rope that was attached to the entrance hall table. It allowed him to walk no farther than the front door until he learned that was his boundary. In addition, Damyn sought out the grounds crew in Upper Chula Vista and gave them a bottle of tequila to remind them that if they saw tequila, they should bring him home.

Tequila has been at home with Damyn and John ever since his escape to San Antonio Tlayacapan. They have moved from Upper Chula Vista to Riberas de Pilar and Tequila feels at home there as well. Damyn's father now has the Upper Chula Vista house, so Tequila visits there when Damyn and John travel.

Tequila has been patrolling that big mountain top property since he was a year old, and he continues to do so when he visits Damyn's father. The difference now is that he's slowed down with the passage of years. When he comes home to Riberas he's so tired he sleeps for three days.

Party Animal

I'm Tequila. I got my name because I met my forever family at a Christmas party. It's a perfect name because I do love to party! When I hear the cork pop from the wine bottle and the glasses tinkling, I'm ready. Let me tell you how I work a room.

My favorite game is chase the tennis ball. Here's the way I play it. I leave the ball in the general vicinity of a person I want to play with. Then I go hide behind a chair or a bush close to the patio. Someone always picks the ball up and throws it. That's when I appear in a streak across the grass and get the ball. See, they don't know where I am so it always amazes them.

I notice as humans drink wine their attention span sometimes shortens, so I have to keep everyone on alert. If the person who has been throwing the ball stops, I choose someone else and give them the opportunity. Parties at our house are fabulous! And it only takes one guest to make a party for me.

Once many years ago I went exploring out beyond our property wall. I don't do that anymore. Haven't for years. As a result of that, Damyn got tiny flashlights in different colors. When my friends come in the evening with their huMans, each of us gets our own color flashlight attached to our harnesses. That way our huMans can always know where we are in the black, black night outside.

I guess you've read about how I disappeared a few times right after I came to live with Damyn and John. I had a home. I don't remember too much about it after all these years. I just remember I had one. I was there for what seemed like a long time and no one came home. The food was gone. There was no water. I jumped over the fence to see if I could find my family...or at least some food.

So when Damyn and John brought me to their house after the party, I felt like I still needed to find my own place where I belonged. It didn't take me long to figure out I belonged wherever Damyn and John were. They would never let me be hungry or thirsty.

Yes, thank you, I'd love another treat.

I'll admit to a kind of wandering spirit even after I settled in here. I know my limits, where my boundaries are, and I honor them. I love to play at the house we shared when I first came to live with Damyn and John. It has a big hole in the ground that's full of water. There are some steps leading into the water. Sometimes I go stand on the top step. That's as far as I go. The fountain is a different story. It's my favorite place to cool off when the days get hot in the late spring before the rains come.

Patrolling that property takes a lot out of me. I'm glad I don't have to do it all the time the way I used to. Our new house is a lot less work, and the parties are just as much fun. You could say I enjoy the best of both worlds. Because I do.

Only 97 More to Go...

Rick and Heidi arrived in Lakeside from Phoenix, Arizona, in 2002. They adopted a dog, Abby, who enjoyed her position as an only dog. She seemed to be getting spoiled, so they started looking for another dog. The day before the Animal Shelter closed, they drove over to find one. They wanted a female, preferably a Schnauzer type because Heidi has allergies. They were done with puppies...too high maintenance.

At the shelter, Heidi was nearly bowled over by the eager dogs wanting a home. At first she didn't see the little black PLT (Poodle-Like-Thing) that walked over to her slowly, elegantly, and deliberately. Heidi reached down, picked her up and the dog planted a big wet kiss on Heidi's cheek. This was their dog. They named her Cydney after a very dear friend who is like their daughter… and because she had big feet, like their friend Cydney.

The name almost caused a scandal. One day, shortly after Cydney (the dog) had joined the household, a friend told Rick he was looking tired. Rick explained that he couldn't get a full night's sleep because all Cydney wanted to do was play all night. The friend's eyebrows shot up and Rick realized how it sounded. He explained about the name before the story had a chance to go any further.

Abby accepted Cydney in a tolerant sort of way.

Once, while Heidi was away in Europe, Rick was missing her. One of their customers thought Rick needed a dog to cheer him up. She already had three at home and Rick didn't want to hurt the feelings of a well-intentioned gift so he took her home. She wasn't much to look at and had fleas. On the way Rick stopped at Dr. Memo's to get her a flea bath.

Rick was still moping, and wasn't feeling much of anything for the new dog. Until about the third day when he came home and found a toy explosion in the house... he fell in love. Any stray with the creativity and initiative to find the entire collection of dog toys, and spread them all over the house to make a statement, was worth his attention.

Rick tried brushing her to make her a little more presentable. She looked lovely for about an hour and then her hair reverted to its natural mess. He decided the only name for her would be Scruffy.

There's enough love for everyone... and more.

Rick picked up Heidi at the airport and did not mention the addition to the family until they were stepping in the door. Of course, all the dogs were waiting to greet them... tails wagging, barking, jockeying for attention. Rick picked up Scruffy, handed her to Heidi and said, "This is your new Mommy." Something happened between Heidi and Scruffy at that moment and they have been practically inseparable ever since.

Abby was the oldest dog in the house and did not appreciate the addition of Scruffy. In fact, she tried to terrorize Scruffy every day, until the day she died. They decided not to actively look for another dog. They would just wait until one came along that met their requirements.

One day a lady from Lucky Dogs Rescue told them about a cute little Poodle. Rick and Heidi looked at each other and within an hour, they were at Lucky Dog to meet her. It turns out she is a Standard Poodle with long elegant legs. And she was standing beside a Chihuahua, which made her look even taller.

She had just been groomed and looked gorgeous...irresistibly gorgeous, actually. She went home with them and is called Yuki after another dear friend.

Truth be told, Rick and Heidi would have 100 dogs if they could.

Freedom's Just Another Word

I was living on the streets, minding my own business when one day a human picked me up and took me to a place where other dogs lived… in cages. We were barking back and forth to each other. I was trying to find out what this place was and why anyone would want to give up freedom to be here. It turns out "here" was only temporary. All the other dogs wanted humans to come and take them to a house. So every time a human walked in, they'd all start barking and jumping and wagging their tails… trying to get a human's attention. Not me. I was waiting for a chance to get back to my streets.

Finally, I had a plan. I'd be nice to some humans who would take me to their house and I could escape from there. Almost immediately, opportunity knocked. A man and lady walked in. All the other dogs started with the barking, jumping and attention seeking. I just looked at the humans and slooooowly walked towards them… not barking… not flapping my tail in the wind. I would be elegant about it. Living on the streets didn't mean I had no class.

The lady picked me up… I started to lick her face because humans seem to like that. Oh yeah, she was laughing and hugging me. My strategy had worked!

They took me to a place that had a fence around it. I checked it out, and it looked like it might be easy to jump over. I checked out the rest of the garden, looking for potential escape hatches. There were a few places that had possibilities. I'd work on the escape plan later.

Another dog, named Abby, lived there too. She was old and didn't want to play with me. Her loss, I thought. I'm not taking her when I leave.

After I'd been playing for a while, the huMan says to me, "Let's go inside." Now, I didn't know what "inside" meant so I just followed him until we came to this wall that he opened. I skidded to a stop. Nope, not goin' in. I don't know what's in there. Or how to get out. That would only complicate my plan.

My life is so much better than my plan.

The lady brought me some food and water. I was hungry so I ate and drank it all. She said, "You want more?" and picked me up and took me through that wall. I wriggled and jumped out of her arms and was outside before the wall closed! Whew, close call. I just laid down and fell asleep. I'd had a busy day and I could further my plan tomorrow.

Well the next day turned into another day and another. And our huMom as I call her, makes delicious food. She sits next to me and feeds me this cold, smooth stuff. It's soooooo yummy. That's how she finally lured me "inside." She kept picking me up and taking me in and after a while I realized it was OK in there. That's where the stuff she calls "ice cream" is.

What about my plan? Yeah, well… plans change, you know?

197

They Like Me... They Really Like Me

I think I was a puppy when I came to live here. I don't remember a family... human or dog. I think I was alone a lot. I do remember my first few days here. There was a huMan and two other dogs. The huMan didn't seem very happy. He didn't talk to me much. He didn't play with me much. In fact he didn't seem too interested in me at all.

I needed to get his attention and make him like me. One day while he was away, I gathered up all the toys I could find... there were lots... and I just started throwing them in the air and moving them around and leaving them all over. When he came back he said, "Wow, a toy explosion! Come here you." I thought maybe he was mad and I was in trouble. Then he got down on the floor and started wrestling with me and laughing. Whew... he liked me after all. We still roll around on the floor together... it's one of our special things. Sometimes the other dogs join in.

Oh yeah, the other dogs. One was called Abby. She was old and cranky and she didn't like me at all. I couldn't do anything right in her eyes. She would bark at me and chase me and taunt me. She would push me away from my food. I don't know what her problem was. I was a cute, little white fluffy puppy that just wanted to be liked. I wanted her to play with me. She made me nervous. I was really scared of her. I got this itchy rash. And then my hair started to fall out. My beautiful white curls were everywhere, except on me.

It's a good thing the other dog, Cydney, was nice to me. We became sisters and friends because we both didn't like that Abby. Cydney told me Abby was mean to her too.

I wasn't too sad when she crossed over the Rainbow Bridge. The best thing I can say about her is she changed my life... well, my appearance anyway. When my hair grew back I didn't have curls anymore! And my hair isn't white! I'm now a coarse-haired auburn cutie.

Our huMom is awesome. The first time I met her, I jumped into her arms and started kissing her. I figured I'd take the direct approach to make her like me. She really liked it and she was kissing me right back. I'm kind of like her little baby. She protects me. When Abby used to get particularly mean she would tell her to leave me alone. Abby would give me a mean look and bare her teeth and then walk away.

I'm too pretty to be called Scruffy, right?

I like to play. The huMan likes to play with me too. He holds on to one end of a pool noodle and I pull on the other end and shake my head. I try to get it away from him and he tries to get it away from me. I really like that game.

A new dog came to join our family. Her name is Yuki and she's huge. I was afraid of her at first. Turns out she's just as much fun as Cydney and our huMan. We all play together all day. She's like another sister and she likes me too.

At night we all go to bed together with our humans. We all roll around. It's a real dog pile with arms and legs and paws and tails all over the place. When it's time for sleeping, I go to the living room and sleep on the sofa. I like to sleep alone.

I also like my home and my family… and they all like me too.

Food, Glorious Food

I was living in a place called "Lucky Dogs." Seriously? What's so lucky about a lot of barking and no privacy and really bland food? I had one friend, Chichi the Chihuahua. She was so little; she was more like a toy. I'm a Standard Poodle and very few dogs measure up to me.

Just after my bath one day, I was strolling around, letting my hair fluff dry in the sun. Chichi was huffing and puffing and running along beside me. Some humans came in. They looked around like they were confused. Then Bob, one of the nice humans, brought them over to me. The lady said, "Oh my gosh, she's gorgeous" and I knew they were talking about me. I huddled up to them and they were petting me and the next thing I knew, Bob was telling me to say good-bye to Chichi.

We got in a car and I put my paw on the window to wave to Chichi. She'd be OK. She's cute and makes friends easily. I was off to a new adventure.

We got to the human's house and guess what? They had toy dogs for me to play with! I thought, "I'm going to like it here." There's Cydney… she's not actually overweight, just a little under tall. She's really friendly and she teaches me stuff… like going outside to pee and then going to the bedroom to wait for the humans to go to bed.

There's another dog the humans call Scruffy… good name. Her hair is a mess. Turns out, she's well named because she loves to run and play and have fun… and her hair gets all messed up. We became friends right away.

I haven't even gotten to the best part yet.

The HuMom is a really good cook and she makes us the most scrumptious smelling and tasting food. Before she feeds us, she takes a few bites to make sure it's not too hot and it won't upset our tummies. I watched the humans eat so I would know what to do… I wanted to make a good impression. I picked up my piece of meat and took it to the place where they were eating. I jumped on a chair and put my food on the table in front of me. Just like them. I looked at them and started eating my food, in small bites, so I didn't make a mess. When I was done, I jumped down. They were laughing so I guess I did the right thing.

In this home we are *all* lucky dogs

I did make one eating mistake. It was dinnertime and I was hungry after a long day of running around with Cydney and Scruffy. I flew in the house and smelled something delectable. It was already on the table. I jumped up and started eating off the plate. I didn't know where the humans were. I was so busy eating I really didn't care that much. Until the huMan came in and said, "What are you doing?" Ooooops, it seems I ate their food.

I like to watch TV with Cydney. We just sit and look at the animals. We can watch for hours. My favorites are the dogs. Sometimes Cydney gets curious and she looks behind the TV when we hear the dogs barking. She hasn't found any yet. I think she's wasting her time.

Cydney and Scruffy are more than just toys. They're my friends and my sisters. The humans love us and laugh with us. We all eat very well. This is a pretty cool family. Huh, I guess I am a lucky dog!

A Dream Fulfilled

Rachel McMillen and her dog, Zack, first came from Vancouver Island to the village of Ajijic in 2009. They returned every year for several months at a time before permanently relocating in 2013. Rachel volunteered at the Spay and Neuter ranch and made the decision that once she moved here, she would adopt dogs. She found a property large enough to comfortably accommodate four smallish dogs, which was her dream.

Soon after she and Zack arrived in 2009, Rachel's neighbor noticed an emaciated, wounded small black dog in the vacant lot across the street from her home. She named the little female Poodle mix Sami, and took her into her home… to the immediate distaste of one of her other dogs. She called Rachel and implored her to take Sami at least long enough to nurse her back to health.

When Rachel and Sami met, the little creature stuck to her chest. That was in 2009. In 2013, Sami still clings to Rachel's chest, or to her lap, or to any other part of her body that she can hold onto. She snuggles every morning with her paws around Rachel's neck.

Zack did not take kindly to Sami, preferring his status as "only" dog. He's bigger than she is and attempted to let her know she was not welcome on his turf. Little, cuddly Sami quickly set him straight. Now they are best friends.

Rachel, a busy and successful mystery writer, says of Sami, "She's slowed me down a lot. I needed that." She also says that Sami has made her even more sensitive to street dogs. The expansion of her brood is certainly testament to that!

In January 2013, Rachel went to Anita's with a friend who had been called there to look at a dog for possible adoption. While Rachel waited for her friend, she noticed a small dog with a huge wound. Her injuries were consistent with those inflicted by dogs trained to fight. She had been found bleeding on the street. When her eyes met Rachel's, there was nothing left to discuss. My max is four dogs, Rachel thought, and I have only two. Dog number three had found her forever home that day with Rachel, Sami, and Zack.

Living the dream

Rachel likes to let dogs grow into their names. She watches to see which one resonates. When she tried Lucy on this three-year-old newest addition, the dog came to her. So Lucy she is.

Lucy is the most playful of Rachel's brood, always trying to engage the others. Her massive wounds indicate to Rachel that she's been abused by other dogs for a long time. That, and her timid and submissive nature, led Rachel to believe that Lucy has lived on the street for most of her life and has always been bullied.

Lucy has been slow to warm to humans. Very gradually, Rachel helped her to learn that it's safe to be cuddled and petted. Sami is the role model for that learning process. As Lucy's life unfolds, she chases cats and seems to have fun playing with toys.

The fourth member of Rachel's canine clan had been acquired as a child's toy. She was thrown out of her home when the child lost interest. Neighbors dropped her off at Anita's two days later. They were leaving the country and could not keep her. She was two months old when Rachel saw her… with her head against the wall and looking depressed. She has had a forever home with Rachel since mid-May of 2013.

Very timid and needy, Lucy is gradually finding her voice, which she uses with Zack when he snatches her chew toy. She prefers to be carried everywhere, so she declines to go walking on the beach with Rachel and the other dogs.

Rachel is happy with her brood of four. They bring humor and delight to each other and to her every day.

Lucky Lucy

When you're a small dog alone on the streets of Chapala, just staying alive is a challenge. I'd been doing that successfully for what felt like a long time. I measure success by whether I wake up after darkness gets washed away by light from the sky.

Darkness is the scariest time. There aren't many humans around and the other street dogs seemed always to find places to hide from the darkness. I wasn't very skilled at that.

One night I was skittering through a dark and empty street when a man came around the corner and grabbed me with his big hand. He threw me into one of those things I always tried to avoid in the streets during the day. It goes along the street on round things that seem to move it. I was so scared, I hid as far away from him as I could. When the thing stopped, he grabbed me and took me into a building.

I had never heard such noise! Dogs were barking and whining and crying? Some of them were attached to long clangy loopy things. I saw them pulling to get away. The clanging and the barking and the whining and the crying made my whole body shake. I was so scared!

When the man put me down I ran, looking for a place to hide. I was successful, too...for a time. Then some dogs came looking for me. I ran. They chased. I got bitten a lot of times. Finally, one of the big dogs attached to the loopy thing got free of it. He was after me. And he caught me. I couldn't wriggle away because his jaws were just too strong. He held me tight and shook me.

The next thing I remember was waking up in another noisy place. There were a lot of barking dogs there just talking amongst themselves. A lady was cleaning my wounds and putting smelly stuff in them that made them feel better. It was while

I was lying quietly and letting my body heal that I first saw Rachel. She had the most loving, beautiful eyes. I felt safe looking at them.

I truly am one lucky dog!

Rachel brought me home and took care of me as I healed. Sami made me feel welcome right away. Zack was a little aloof and that was okay. He never once tried to hurt me.

All of my wounds have healed now. Sami and I love to play together. She jumps on me, I chew her ear, we get so tangled in each other it's hard to tell who's who. Sometimes I see a cat on the wall around our house and I give it a good chase. To tell you the truth, I don't know what I'd do with it if I caught it. It's the chase that's the point of the game.

I love my home and my life with Rachel, Zack, and Sami. Recently, Maggie Mae joined us, too. She'll have to tell you her story. My story can be summed up in one word. "Lucky." Lucky to be alive. Lucky to be living here. Lucky to sleep peacefully at the foot of Rachel's bed in the darkness. And lucky to see the light of the sky from behind the safety of our walls.

New Girl in Town

Rachel calls me Maggie Mae. Most of the time. Sometimes she calls me Worm. That's 'cause I wriggle a lot. I was only two months old when Rachel and I met. I was so depressed. I hadn't seen my Mom since I was about a month old. Then I lived for a time with a little girl who seemed not to know I was a dog.

She put clothes on me and tried to get me to sit in a chair at a table in her room. Then she'd take the clothes off and put on different ones and try to get me to ride on a thing made of wood that rocked. I had all the clothing I needed covering my whole body all the time. I was a puppy not a toy. It wasn't long before I was set out on the street to fend for myself.

I was so tiny it didn't take long for some humans to notice me, feel sorry for me, and pick me up. They couldn't let me live with them because they were going away, so they took me to a place where a lot of lonely dogs live. I felt really sad.

I was lying on the floor with my head against the nice cool wall trying to figure it out. Why was I even born? Doesn't anybody want me? Then Rachel showed up! She scooped me up and cooed at me and held me against her neck. Soon we were on our way to her house.

When we got there, I met Zack, Sami, and Lucy. They were all lots bigger than me, so Rachel carried me everywhere until they got to know me. I liked that! I still do. Even though we're all good friends now, I still make Rachel carry me everywhere. The other dogs go for walks on the beach. I won't because Rachel doesn't carry me.

I'm home now and I know it. I love to play with toys. Chew toys are my favorites. Sometimes Zack will grab one of my chew toys. I really bark at him until he puts it down. In fact, I've put that guy in his place on more than one occasion since I came here.

I've gone in the car with Rachel and the others a couple of times. I just curl up on her shoulder and snuggle in next to her neck. The thing is, my tummy gets all topsy turny-over in the car and then it empties itself out of my mouth and onto Rachel's lap. Rachel says I can go in the car when I'm older and over that.

"Worm?" Yeah. That's me!

Meanwhile, I'm a happy puppy loving life in my new home. My questions have been answered. Rachel wants me… and I was born to be family with Zack, Sami, and Lucy.

Sami the Velcro Dog

If you're looking for me, you'll likely find me clinging to my Rachel someplace. I especially like to hang on her neck...or stick to her chest...or cling to her lap. Anyplace on Rachel that I can get a paw-hold, I'm there.

It seems a long time ago now that I was alone in a vacant lot on a street corner here in Ajijic. I must have been about a year old. I'd been in a fight and had gotten hurt too bad to find food. I was feeling so dizzy I could hardly make out the nice lady who came across the street to check on me. Later I learned her name was Patty.

Seeing I was in a bad way, Patty took me into her house. She gave me food and water and I began to feel better right away. She even gave me a name. Sami. I'd never had a name. It made me feel special. Patty had two dogs. One of them took an immediate dislike to me. I wasn't there long enough to find out the reason. Patty called her friend Rachel to see if I could stay with her until I got well.

I almost didn't want to get well. I didn't want to go back out on the street to live. I liked the way Patty took care of me. I wanted to let Rachel know that I really love living indoors with humans. As soon as I went to live with Rachel, I locked my front legs and paws around her and wouldn't let go.

She gets it. I go everywhere with her and Zack, even on long rides to a place where it's lots cooler than it is here. Zack. Let me tell you about Zack. When I first got well enough to move around in the house, finding my way, settling in, Zack came upon me with a lot of grouchy growling about how he's in charge and he's the "only dog" around here. I had to kick his curly butt just one time. Zack's a smart dog. He got it. Now we're very best friends.

Seems it wasn't all that long ago when Lucy came to live with us. Boy, had she ever been through it! The stories that girl tells make my fur stand straight out from my body. In spite of it all, she loves to play with Zack and me. She and I wrestle all the time. Rachel just laughs and laughs.

Even I have to get down to eat.

Lucy doesn't take any guff off my good friend Zack, either. Poor Zack. Thought he was such a prince. He's my buddy and I love him. I love everybody where I live with Rachel. And I never let her forget that I want to be here with her forever.

Christmas Past and
a Christmas Present

A bit of an iconic figure in the Lake Chapala area, Judy King is best known for her writing and editing achievements... have you heard of the former e-zine and now book, Lake Chapala Living? Or, read the Chapala Review perhaps? Coming from California, she has lived in Lakeside since 1990, when it really was a sleepy, dusty village on the lake. In 2012 she began to parlay her culinary skills into a line of comfort foods with charming stories from Iowa, her original home state. She sells her brand of Homestead Home Cooking products at the Monday Market in Ajijic.

Lesser known as a rescue huMom, Judy is never without loyal companions. Her dear pair of black Labs, Molly and Maggie, came from Anita's Animals. Sadly, in April 2011, they became victims of a serial poisoner who was terrorizing Ajijic. Judy's girls died within an hour of each other, leaving her lonely and bereft.

In June 2011, a friend of Judy's was visiting. Judy was telling her the tragic tale of the loss of her two best friends. She knew she wanted another dog... medium sized... and she had always been drawn to Labs. Before she knew it, she and her friend were in the car and on the way to Anita's.

There was a black Lab and Rotweiller cross that had just come in. It had always lived alone in a condo. It did not know anything about cars, leashes, grass... or other dogs. Definitely a challenge. Judy felt that to look into those eyes every day would be sooooooo worth it. After hours of help from Art Hess, the local dog whisperer, the education and socialization of Milagros Rosario, now known as Mili, was nearly complete. Work continues with Carlos, the dog walker.

Judy ran into Art on Christmas Eve, 2011. She was in an outdoor restaurant as he was walking past with a pack of dogs. He stopped for a chat. Judy asked him, "Do you think I should get my dog a dog for Christmas?" She told him what her specifications were… small, cute, white, fluffy, like Benji, the dog in the movies. He replied, "The dog's needs are more important than yours," as he walked away. Hmmmmmmmmm… wise gift-giving words.

Judy King... writer, editor, chef... *and huMom*

That evening she went to the services at St. Andrew's Anglican Church. Just outside the gate was a dirty, smelly, scruffy miserable looking creature that somewhat resembled a Wheaton Terrier and Poodle mixture. Judy made eye contact and a special feeling passed between her and the dog. After the service was over, the dog had disappeared.

Christmas morning, Judy was back at church. Not for the service… she was looking for that sweet dog. No one seemed to know where it was. One of the parishioners, Steve Cole, heard Judy describe the dog. He immediately got in his car and drove up and down all the streets of Riberas del Pilar until he found it.

He surprised Judy with a special delivery that Christmas afternoon.

As she bathed the dog, Judy remembered a story of a Christmas past. In1973, her daughter, Susannah, received a doll for Christmas. When asked what the doll's name would be she replied, "Why, Merry Christmas, of course."

And for this Christmas present, that was the perfect name.

Comforts of Home

Life can really surprise you.

I remember living a quiet life in a small space. Just me and sometimes some humans. I never went out anywhere. I knew where everything was. It was a quiet life of eating and sleeping. Very routine. Very safe. And very comfortable.

One day, everything changed. Something tight was put around my neck… I feel like I'm choking and a human is pulling me. We go outside of our space and… wait a minute… we're outside our space. I've never been outside. Now he's huffing and puffing and lifting me up and putting me in something. There's a loud noise… slam. I'm lying on something soft that's kind of nice. Then there's a noise and we start moving. I'm trying to stay still because I'm shaking. I can't get my balance. I'm afraid and I feel like I might fall. The moving stops. I get lifted out. I hear a lot of dogs barking. I'm wondering where are we?

Now I'm standing on something rough that hurts my feet. I gingerly walk a bit and now there's something tickle-y on my feet. I'm still shaking because I'm soooooooo scared. I'm looking around everywhere. I don't recognize anything. What the heck is going on? Where did all these dogs come from? What am I supposed to do?

The human left and I didn't like being in a place with so many dogs. It was noisy all the time. I had to look for water. The food wasn't the warm and delicious food I used to get. My special bowls were gone. Dogs were barking at me and running around me and sniffing me and…well, I just didn't know what to do. I could never get any privacy. I didn't like this place whatever it was.

Lucky for me I was only there a short time. Two ladies were looking at me and nodding their heads. Someone put something around my neck and I was thinking oh no, here we go again.

I was back in one of those moving things. It wasn't quite as scary the second time. When we stopped, we went inside... where I felt comfortable. It was very quiet. I went under a table and lay down and just sighed. I was exhausted from all this change and trauma. That night the lady named Judy called me to get up on her bed. Whew. This felt better and more familiar. Maybe this would be OK.

I love a good surprise.

The next day a man came and took me out. He put a thing around my neck...again. He did it very gently. He had a nice soothing voice. He talked to me a lot and taught me stuff... mostly how to not be afraid. After a while he stopped coming. Now, our friend, Carlos comes to take me for a walk.

My Judy is very busy. She cooks a lot. She sits at a table and makes noises by tapping on something. She talks to me and I listen. She tells me I'm a good listener. It seems pretty easy to make Judy happy.

I have a special chair that I like to curl up on and sleep while she's so busy. I get upset if Judy puts stuff on my chair. I have to bark to remind her it's my chair. She just laughs and says, "oh, Mili." Sometimes I hop on the couch to sleep. I will sleep almost anywhere, actually… as long as there's a pillow for my head.

Everything's comfortable again and I'm not surprised that this feels like home.

Timing is Everything

I'd been hanging around this big house where lots of people would go in and out. They'd sing and I loved to listen to them. Sometimes they had parties and people would stop and talk to me and give me a bite or two to eat. There was a nice garden too… very peaceful and a good place to sleep. Most days, when no one came to the big house, I wandered the streets looking for food, water and friends.

One night a lady stopped and looked at me at the exact same moment that I looked at her. I felt like I knew her… or I really wanted to get to know her. She just kept walking… into the big house with all the other people. I hung around for a while. I was a little hungry so I went to look around the streets for some scraps. I got tired and fell asleep in a doorway.

Suddenly, I heard a voice say, "It's you" and a man picked me up. I felt a bit rough, my coat was matted and I know I didn't smell like flowers. That didn't seem to bother the man. He took me to a place I'd been before. I got poked and prodded and a man looked in my ears, my eyes and in my… well behind area, you know. Maybe he was looking for why I smelled. He looked in my mouth and then he got this tickly thing and was moving it all over my teeth. I was wiggling because it felt so funny.

Next thing I know, we're on the move again and I end up at a house. A lady is there. She looked at me. I looked at her. And I thought, "It's you" at the exact moment that she said, "It's you!" I knew this lady. I'd wished for her to come back to me. And here we were.

She took a step back… yeah I think I still smelled bad. She was talking to me and laughing and she put me in some warm water with white tickle-y things and rubbed me until I smelled beee-yooo-tee-ful. The lady was hugging me and kissing me and smelling me… and she kept saying "Merry" so I think that's my name now.

She put me on the floor and I started looking around. Uh-oh, I spied another dog. This could be tricky. I just looked at her and stayed away from her. She was chewing on something that sounded tasty. I was watching her. She got up and went outside so I ran over, grabbed it and took it to a quiet place. I started chewing on it and it was good. That other dog came back and just sat in front of me and watched me.

She's pretty nice to me. She shares her toys and chewy things. Not her food though. On no, she's really protective of her food. Her name is Mili.

The lady, her name is Judy, gave me a special blankie… just for me and I don't share it with Mili, the other dog. When I need a nap, I go to my sleeping place, under a table, and I roll around on the blankie and scrunch it up and then I crawl under it. I usually give a big sigh and fall asleep. I love my blankie because it's just mine.

Mili and I have become really good friends. I tease her and get her running around with me. And every day our buddy, Carlos, comes and takes us for a walk. Well almost every day. Actually he didn't come for a few a days and we couldn't figure out what was going on. Every day, like usual, we'd lie down and look at he door and wait. And wait. Then he came to talk to Judy. He had these sticks that he was leaning on. He was kind of hopping and one of his feet was wrapped up. We were so excited to see him that we almost knocked him over. Then we went to the door and waited for him to take us out, like he usually did. Carlos came to the door. His face was sad. He shook his head and said, "Not today, girls." Then he went out the door without us! For a lot of days we waited for Carlos and finally he came back. Now we go for our walk every day.

Our Judy makes the best food ever. When she's in the kitchen the smells are deeee-lish-us! Mili and I watch her very carefully because if something falls on the floor, it's ours.

And speaking of eating, I love to go out to breakfast with Judy. We know the places on the plaza where I can sit with her and she feeds me bacon. She talks to people and I talk to the other dogs. Mili stays home and guards the house. She doesn't like going with us.

It *is* you.

I don't bark much. Mili barks a lot and Judy doesn't like that. I mean a leaf could fall off a tree and she goes crazy barking. I keep telling her… only when a stranger comes. She just gets over-excited I think.

We have so many good times… Mili, Judy, and me. I often think, what if I didn't see Judy that night? All of our lives would be so different.

The Singer, the Actress and The Clown

im moved to Ajiic from the U.S. in late 2005. Early on he developed concern for the many dogs he saw wandering the streets. He and his friend David have always been dog people, so bringing street dogs into their La Floresta home seemed like an easy thing to do.

La Floresta is the Ajijic neighborhood adjacent to San Antonio Tlayacapan. It is home to the local Walmart, Centro Laguna shopping mall with its shops and cinema multiplex, and other businesses frequented by the local community. Getting there from La Floresta is a pleasant walk, which David takes frequently.

One day on the way home from San Antonio Tlayacapan to La Floresta, David saw a pair of puppies crawl out from under the gate of a nearby soccer field. Very small and very determined, they trotted up the road toward him. David scooped them up and carried them home.

After watching their behavior for a while, Jim decided to name them after two of his favorite performers. The little female became Diane Keaton. She's always "on" and she loves to run the show. The male is Hank Williams. Hank sits on the couch and looks cute. He uses his eyes in a special way so it's impossible not to notice how cute he really is.

Neither Hank nor Diane plays with toys. Their entertainment comes, instead, from playing with each other. Even though they emerged from an outdoor safe haven for street dogs, Jim never had to train them. They came through the door housebroken and they rarely bark.

Lucky, on the other hand, is quite mouthy and very rambunctious. David saw her in the street one evening in the spring of 2012 as he walked home from San Antonio. She was rail thin and digging in a trashcan. David quickly went home to get Jim and the car.

It was at that point that she got lucky, and Lucky became her name.

Once in the house, they could see that her coat was matted and faded, her eyes were sunk deep in the sockets and she had obviously been starving for quite a long time. Jim and David saw to her medical needs, had her groomed, and put five kilos on her over the course of the rest of the calendar year.

David laughingly refers to Lucky as a "nut case." She loves to play and grabs David's arm to let him know she wants to wrestle. She and Jim walk twice a day. She's very social, and greets people on the street with a wagging tail and a twinkle in her eye.

With Diane and Hank romping through the back yard, and Lucky frolicking around the front gate, Jim and Dave are constantly entertained. Their funny four-legged friends are family.

Not Quite Famous

I'm Diane Keaton and I'm the star of this show. This is my brother, Hank. *I'm Hank. My job is to sit here and look adorable.*

Diane here again… that's about all you'll get from Hank…for a couple of reasons. One is that he doesn't have much to say. The other is, when he does speak I have to tell him what to say. No, he's not slow or anything like that. He just…well…likes to keep to himself…when he's not chasing me or that stupid Lucky.

Hank has a crush on Lucky. She's about 12 times bigger than he is. She's nice to him…until she sees a butterfly. Then she doesn't even know he's there. She has the attention span of a Milkbone biscuit.

Enough about those two… let me tell you about me. In addition to being cute and adorable, I keep everybody in line around here. I help Jim get our food ready in the morning. No one would eat around here if it wasn't for me. Then I make sure Hank gets enough exercise by running him around the yard a few times a day.

We don't leave the property, Hank and I. We can't. I'm too famous so we'd never be left alone. Actually, Hank's famous, too, although I'm not sure why. I just hear Jim refer to me as a movie star and Hank as a country singer, although I have to tell you, I've never heard a note out of him.

Anyway, when we were puppies living over by the lake, Hank had a really bad experience. He ran off one afternoon and I couldn't find him anyplace. I was really worried because we were very young and didn't have much in the way of street smarts. I couldn't sleep that night. I kept looking for him, patrolling the perimeter of the place we were staying.

Dawn came over the lake and still no Hank in sight. Finally, as the sun rose high in the sky, Hank came wriggling through the bottom of the gate. He looked a mess! I asked him what happened and he wouldn't tell me. He just laid down and slept the rest of the day and all through that night.

Yes, I'm talking to you, Hank. Get in here!

Lucky? Is that you, Lucky?

After that, Hank was different. That's when he started keeping to himself. That's when he stopped talking and I had to start telling him what to say. From then on, I always had to look after Hank. So doing it now… and keeping the rest of these guys in line… is a piece of steak.

One Lucky Lady

efore I came to live with Jim and David, I had another home. I lived with a huMan whose name I don't know because I never heard anybody call him anything. There were two rooms in our house. He lived mostly in one and I lived mostly in the other one.

In the daytime we would sleep late. Then he'd let me out for a walk. I made my rounds getting a bone here and a fresh tortilla there from the local neighborhood. Sometimes I would go to the lake for a swim if a cat didn't need chasing, or a butterfly didn't lead me off in another direction. Whatever I ended up doing, my day had a fun start to it. Every day. Then I'd come home and keep my huMan company. He moved pretty slowly and his fur was mostly gray.

My bed was narrow, long, and had a back he could lean against and arm rests for him on each side. We'd sit together on it in the afternoon and watch a box with shapes on it. Then he'd make supper for us. After supper, I was sleepy and hopped up on the bed in my room. He would come out of his room, walk through mine, and leave through the front door.

Usually it was very late when he came home. He sometimes stumbled through my room on the way to his. I stayed alert in case he needed my help. Other times he'd flop down on my bed beside me, put his hand on my back, and fall asleep.

One morning there was a big commotion in front of our house. Lights were flashing on top of a big white box with wheels on it. Two men came in and put my huMan on a table that also had wheels on it. They rolled him out through the front door. I went after them. They put him in the box and slammed the doors shut before I could get in. The next thing I knew, the white box was rolling away.

I went after it.

On the way, I got sidetracked at a place where I get food. I'd need food for the trip to get my huMan back. So I ate. Then I went for a swim because that's what I always did after I ate. Then there were these two bunny rabbits, so I had to chase them. They parted and I didn't know which one to go after. Then I remembered that I had to find the white box with my huMan in it.

I ran in the direction I'd seen it go. And ran and ran. Pretty soon, I didn't know where I was and I didn't know how to get back. I had to find him or find my home. I wandered for days not knowing where I was or how to get to where I was going. I looked for food. No luck. I looked for water. No luck. I couldn't even find the lake.

C'mon David. Let's play!

After days and days of this, I was exhausted. I felt dizzy. I couldn't even see very well because everything looked fuzzy. That's how I missed the car that pulled up alongside me. Missed it until the passenger door opened and a man held out his hand with something in it that smelled like food. I reached for it and felt his arms around me. The next thing I knew I was in the car. The man was holding me and telling me I was going to be all right.

My luck had changed!

The car drove through a wall into a beautiful grassy place. Two little dogs came running and jumped up to greet me. Well, one greeted me. I later learned his name was Hank. The other one, Diane... she's kind of the boss around here... just looked down her nose at me and then stalked off. I was too weak and tired to take offense.

I got water. Then food. The two men in the car were with me now, talking. I didn't understand most of the words. I drank some more. Ate some more. And went to sleep.

As I got my strength back, I found I really liked the front yard. I could hear everything going on outside our wall. I would hear if the white box drove by. I didn't know how to let David and Jim… that's what they called each other… I didn't know how to let them know I had a missing huMan out there somewhere in a white box.

Diane told me what the rules were. Stay out of her back yard. Don't eat her food or drink her water. And don't chase Hank. She has to settle for two out of three. Hank and I are best buddies and we play together a lot when Hank isn't helping Diane look after the back yard. Of course, I take care of the front.

David and Jim and I go for walks a couple of times a day. I wear a collar now and one of them hooks me up to a long stringy thing that he holds in his hand. It's just the three of us go. Hank and Diane don't go.

Hank is little. Sometimes I want to play a little rougher than I can with Hank. When I do, I just go grab David's arm and get him to play. We wrestle together. I get lots of treats and I've gained so much weight since I moved in here. The food here is way better than what I'd get when I had to go look for it every day.

I've stopped listening for my huMan. He's not coming for me and I couldn't find him. I have a good life now here with David and Jim. I am one lucky girl. In fact, that's what they call me: Lucky.

Famous Last Words

Originally from Chicago, Joni and Rich were living in California in a lovely apartment that did not permit pets. Joni had always had a dog and was pining for one. They were planning to move and she told Rich that as soon as they got to Mexico she was getting a dog.

They arrived Lakeside July 1, 2008. On July 3, before all the boxes were unpacked, Joni was going to the animal shelter to "look." As she went out the door, Rich said, "Don't you dare come home with a dog."

At the shelter, Joni was resolved to be strong. After all, the house was not set up yet and the yard was not fenced. Much had to be done before she could have her dog. She was there just to see what was available.

She came to a large cage with two odd looking puppies in it. They looked alike and they were ugly, not an ounce of cuteness between them… all pink and hairless. They had been shaved due to severe flea infestation. One had long legs and a huge personality. As Joni approached, she began leaping up and down, making eye contact with Joni as if to say, "Take me, take me." The other one just stood on her hind legs, paws on the cage, with a pleadingly hopeful look.

Joni was smitten with both. She just could not decide. They seemed to belong together. The woman at the shelter said, "Why not take both?" That had not occurred to her. Rich had said not to bring home a dog. He couldn't argue with two. She arranged for the shelter to keep the puppies for a couple of days. She went home, told Rich the story and, somehow, he was not surprised.

While continuing to unpack, there was a lot of conversation about what to call the dogs. Of course, their names had to re-flect their nationality… so Chile Pepper and Mexicali Rose were chosen.

He's *so* happy she didn't listen.

When the girls came home they had to stay in the house because the yard was not fenced. They were easy to train, well behaved, loving and fun. They blossomed, literally, as their hair grew in and they turned out to be soft and lovely PLTs (Poodle-Like-Things).

Chile acts older, like the big sister. She protects the super sensitive Mexi. Mexi is a lover and will kiss anyone's face off. If she misbehaves, and is told she is a "bad girl" she is immediately ashamed and slinks off to hide under a bed. Often she needs to be coaxed out.

Chile hides her sensitivity… when caught in the act of doing something she isn't supposed to do, she will give a lop-sided grin, look sheepishly at the floor and seem to be blushing with embarrassment.

Squirt came into the household in July of 2013. She was immediately accepted as the little sister. They all eat together, sleep together (on the bed with Joni and Rich) and play together. None of them care for the swimming pool.

They all care for Joni and Rich (and each other) more than we will ever know.

Sisters

Mexi: Hola, my name is Mexicali Rose and…

Chile: Oh, lah-dee-dah, with the fancy name… I'm her sister, Chile Pepper. Everybody calls me Chile and everybody calls her Mexi and we came to this house after we were…

Mexi: Left in a box outside the Animal Shelter, with our other sister. She jumped out of the box and…

Chile: We haven't seen her since. We miss her and we wonder where she might be. We live in a very pretty house with Joni….

Mexi: And Rich! They feed us, and take us for walks and…

Chile: They take really good care of us. Joni taught us how to behave like ladies. Like when we have to pee…

Mexi: We go outside. Which reminds me of a funny story of when we first got here and…

You never let me… what? Finish?

Chile: Well, it's kind of a funny story. Remember Joni and Rich were a bit mad at us…

Mexi: Yeah, yeah. Well they laugh now when they tell people about when we first moved here...

Chile: And there was no fence outside...

Mexi: So when they had to go away without us...

Chile: They put us in the house and closed the door. We could look out the window...

Mexi: We just couldn't go out and play. We used to sit here...

Chile: Just looking out the window and wishing... sigh... then I had...

Mexi: No I had the bright idea...

Chili: Na-ah, it was me. I noticed that some of the smallish windowpanes on a door were cracked so...

Mexi: One especially pretty day you pushed on one and the glass fell out and we just jumped out and were playing in the yard when Joni and Rich came home.

Chile: Yeah, I think they wanted to be angry... they were just so surprised that...

I had the bright idea...

Mexi: They just held us and told us they loved us and they were so happy we were safe and how did we get outside and…

Chile: Then the next time they went out, they moved that big heavy purple thing in front of the door… huh… so I jumped up on one end.

Mexi: And I hopped up on the other end and we could see out the window. We just couldn't go out. Until I had…

Chile: Nooooooo, I had the idea to…

Mexi: Scratch at the purple thing until it moved. It was so heavy, we both just started scratching…

Chile: And gnawing. And gnawing and scratching. And it seemed to move a little bit…

Na-AH… it was *my* idea to…

Mexi: And then a little bit more… and after a looooooooong time there was enough room for us to scooch outside and lie in the sun…

Chile: Which is where we were when Joni and Rich came home. And this time they were really…

Mexi: Surprised and a little bit more angry. Joni called me a "bad girl" and I was scared so I ran and hid…

Chile: Under the bed… you big baby. She had to go and coax you out. When Rich told me I was a "bad girl" I just put my head down and looked at the floor and then I looked at him with my very saddest eyes and he picked me up and I snuggled him and everything was OK.

Mexi: Hey, do you smell that? I think…

Chile: Oh yeah… Joni is cooking something and it smells yummmmmmmmmmmy.

Mexi: Race you to our bowls… last one there's a…

I Think I Love Him

It was a hot and dusty day and I was hungry and thirsty. I had this really heavy thing around my neck and it was following behind me. My neck hurt. My skin was itchy. Every time a car passed me on the street I would stop and sit… hoping someone would pick me up… and watch it go by. I really needed help. I was starting to feel weak. I was only six months old and I didn't have a lot of strength.

I was lying down, taking a little rest when a huMan got out of a car and he had something that smelled really yummy in his hand. I started to go close to him and I then I thought what if he was a bad guy… and was going to catch me… and hurt me… and not let me go… or… maybe not. Whatever he had sure smelled good and I was soooooooooo hungry. I took a chance and went very close to him and in his hand was something to eat. I licked everything out of that hand and then licked it one more time, to thank him for his kindness. He walked towards his car and I followed him, hoping for more to eat. He gently lifted me into the car. I didn't smell very nice so I was surprised he let me in.

He was talking to me with a quiet, gentle voice. He took me to a place where another huMan looked at me and poked me and he kept turning his head away because of my smell. I was embarrassed and I kept very still. He got a machine that made a noise and started to rub it all over my body and my hair all fell off! Then a lady put me in some water and rubbed me and rubbed me and rubbed me and I started to feel better… and smell much better.

My neck still hurt and I had some bad scratches where I'd tried to make the itching stop. The huMan put some sticks in me. Finally, I was so exhausted; I just let out a big sigh and laid down for a sleep.

I think I love him. Actually, I *know* I love him.

I woke up in that car again. And there was a little pile of food right beside me. My kind huMan had left it for me for when I woke up. I think I love him.

When we got out of the car, I was feeling much better. I looked kind of funny with no hair. That didn't matter to Mexi and

Chile. They're the other girls in the house and they look like me, well like me with hair. They're bigger because they're older. They both licked me and we rolled around on the floor and started playing.

Now I have water to drink, food to eat, sisters to play with and some really nice people who take care of me… especially that huMan. He calls me Squirt, I guess because I'm the littlest one, and he smiles at me when he says it. He hugs me lots. And I lick his face, very softly. I think I love him.

I'm still learning how to do stuff. Mexi and Chile are teaching me. They're really good big sisters. And the lady of the house is teaching me too. Sometimes I just get tired and I can't remember everything. Like I go in this box and then they let me out and we go outside and someone says "pee" or "poop." Well I don't always have to pee. I poop outside because it smells yucky and I've had enough of bad smells. Sometimes when I really, really have to go, I pee in the house and then the people tell me I'm a bad dog… and Mexi and Chile just slink away when they hear that. So much for sisterhood. One day I'll remember that outdoors is for pooping and peeing.

I like everything about this place and everyone who lives here. Rich, that's my huMan, saved my life so I stay close to him and watch his every move. He likes to be close to me too. He smiles at me all the time. He tells me I'm pretty… now that my hair is growing back. Whenever I can, I jump on his lap and settle in and he rubs my tummy. I let out a big sigh. I *know* I love him.

A Place for Paco

Tim and Arlene Schubert moved to Ajijic in 2009 and had been sharing their home with their large dogs, Addie and Margo, and Lolita the cat. Daisy came to live with them in May of 2012. Daisy was a delightful and welcome addition to their home and their lives. So when she died in February of 2013, Arlene wanted another dog.

Yes, Tim. I think you're right. I'll tell the others.

Arlene heard about Paco from a woman friend, who said he was an adorable horse hair Shar Pei. She also said he'd been living for two months in a cage at Dr. Pepe Magaña's. "Pepe," as he's known in Lakeside, is a veterinarian in Riberas del Pilar who often takes in injured homeless dogs. Arlene went to Pepe's to meet Paco.

One of Paco's front legs had been severely injured and was

twisted beyond his ability to use it at all. Arlene found it difficult to get him out of his kennel because he was so afraid. After successfully coaxing him out, she just sat with him for an hour, petting him all over. He was calm and sweet, and not at all cowardly. Arlene and Tim took him home.

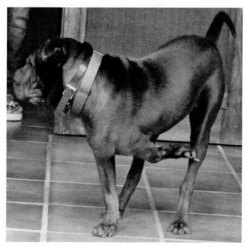

Could this *be* more annoying?

For the first couple of nights, Paco cried all night in his kennel. During the day he chewed socks and all the velcro off of a $140 pair of athletic shoes. Tim and Arlene thought he was depressed. Then they realized he was just a little insecure with two other big dogs and a cat in his new environment. With love and attention, he got over that pretty quickly.

Within the first week, Paco was the alpha dog in the house. Addie and Margo left Lolita alone completely until Paco joined the family. His strong prey drive sent him after her several times a day. And because he was leader of the pack, Margo and Addie joined him on the chase.

Determined to maintain peace in the compound, Lolita was assigned a safe place to be where the dogs were not. Meanwhile, Lakeside trainer, Art Hess, taught Paco to leave Lolita alone. He also introduced additional socialization and in-home manners that have enhanced Paco's popularity with family and guests alike.

At 11 months, Paco and Lolita could be in the same room and

he would not even notice her.

The cause of Paco's leg injury was unknown to anyone connected with his rescue. Tim and Arlene took him to an orthopedic surgeon in Guadalajara who said the nerves in his leg were not responsive. There was no way to correct his deformed and useless leg. Amputation surgery was recommended in order to give him balance.

Following surgery and a very few days of adjustment, Paco enjoys an active, happy life on three legs. Still the alpha dog, he keeps Addie and Margo happy and brings joy and delight to the hearts of Tim and Arlene.

Three is My Lucky Number

My name's Paco and three is my lucky number. Let me tell you why. It all started when I was just a little pup at home with my Mom and my brothers and sisters. I was curious and really strong, even as a little squirt, so I went off exploring long before it was a good idea.

I was just walking along looking at stuff when my front leg got caught in something. I don't know what it was. I just know it was stuck in here. I wriggled and struggled and twisted and pulled until I finally got it out. Boy did it hurt! I couldn't stand up on it.

About that time, Mom came and found me. She latched onto the scruff of my neck and hauled me back home where I belonged. She wasn't mad at me like I thought she'd be. She just kissed my leg over and over and she cried a little bit, too. Seems like when we pups are hurt, our Moms hurt, too.

After a while, my leg stopped hurting. Even so, it was always swinging around in front of me. I could never get it to go on the ground. I had a hard time standing up because, well, there was this space where my paw should be on the ground. I've heard it said that youngsters are resilient. We just bounce right back. I don't know about the bouncing part. I do know I was able to stay upright as I got older.

One day I got taken away from my Mom. All my brothers and sisters had gone off to forever homes. I wasn't chosen. So a person who lived in my house took me to Dr. Pepe's. He was sad that he couldn't fix my leg. When no one came back to pick me up, he gave me a place to sleep and food and water every day. I felt alone. As daylight and darkness came and went many times, I got scared. What if nobody ever comes back for me? What will happen to me?

I was having those feelings when a sweet, sweet woman came to my kennel and spoke to me. I didn't know her. She seemed nice enough. Still, I was unsure whether to allow her to touch me.

After a long time, I came out of the kennel and we just sat together outdoors. I loved it! She rubbed me all over. I especially liked it when she rubbed my tail. That felt soooooo good! It wasn't long after that when she and Tim, another human, came and got me and took me to their house.

Oh my goodness! There were two really big dogs there, and me with this bad leg swinging around uncontrollably. How will I take care of myself? I just stayed in my kennel and cried. Sometimes I would go out with Tim. Just the two of us. When we came back, Addie, the big brindle dog, just looked at the door. No way I was crossing that threshold, with or without Tim. Finally, Addie would walk away and I'd slip back into the house. I found comfort in chewing socks and shoes.

Ah, much better. Thank you!

There was another creature who lived in the house. Not a dog. Furry. Quick. I had to get it. I forgot all about my fear and took off after it. It was really fast! I never did catch it. Pretty soon Addie, and the big black Poodle, Margo, were joining me in the chase. They chose me as the leader of the pack because I was clearly the great hunter among us. It was the beginning of "The Three Amigos." We had a great time together. We still do.

About that furry critter: Arlene...she's the sweet woman who came to visit me at Dr Pepe's and brought me here to the house she shares with Tim...Arlene calls it a cat. She also says we can't chase it and she put it away someplace where we couldn't get it.

Then this really cool human named Art came to the house. He has a way of helping me to understand how much better my life will be here if I just do what the humans want me to do. He explains how reasonable their requests are. He shows me how we can all get along with each other and with other humans who come to visit. I like Art. There are always treats available when Art's here.

The leg I was telling you about is still a problem at this point. I get around okay. It's just that I'm getting bigger and this useless limb flopping back and forth in front of me is throwing me off balance. I went with Tim and Arlene to see a doctor far away from our house. I didn't understand all the words.

Sometime after that, we went back to the same place. We went into a room that had a really strange smell and felt colder than the room we'd come out of. I felt a prick in my shoulder and then I guess I fell asleep. When I woke up, that leg was nowhere to be seen. Wow! What a relief.

I was wrapped in white stuff where the leg used to be and I felt a little sore there for a few days. Almost as soon as we got back home, I could walk better. Now I run around all over the place with Addie and Margo just as graceful as you please. I'm the one of The Three Amigos with three legs. I guess you could say three's my lucky number.

Oh, and the cat? Haven't seen her.

Who's Who

OUR THANKS...

This book would not have made it to your hands without the help and support of many caring and talented humans.

Our heartfelt thanks, hugs (and licks from Winston and Luna) go out to our dear friends:

Pam Harting —for the second time, her attention to detail makes us look good. We couldn't do it without you, Pam.

Shirley Thayer—her really good camera and even better eye makes everything look good.

I'm Winston and I rescued Valerie.

We'll be making our donations to Alianza por una Educación Humanitaria for their education program, GUARDIANS OF THE PLANET. Currently being offered in 51 schools in Jalisco state, the program promotes respect toward all living beings with whom we share the planet.

ESPERA means "Wait!" and is the acronym for the program lesson dedicated to responsible care of animales de compañía. The message: If you plan to get a companion animal, please WAIT! First you need,

Educación
Salud
Protección
Esterilización
Respeto
Adopción

The word *pet* is no longer used to describe the relationship between the animal and the family. This newly educated generation influences families and communities with the posters and other projects they produce in class. The multiplier effect is expected to produce major changes in animal welfare for future generations.

I'm Luna and I rescued Barbara.

Our donation is going to Operación Amor. This is a project to help our limited-income Mexican friends and neighbors who care about their pets and the street dogs (and cats!) in their barrios. The goal is to reduce the number of animals who are having too many babies with no one to look after them. Veterinarians from Mexico City, Guadalajara and Lakeside volunteer their time to perform surgeries at no cost to the families. It began in 2011 and as of September 2013, seven clinics have been held and over 800 operations have been completed. We are proud to support our neighbors in making a difference to reduce the number of homeless animals in our area.

Of course, *Who Rescued Who: Tales of Street Dogs and The People Who Love Them* continues to fund the work of Animal Buddies and ARDAT (the Ajijic Rotary Dog Assist Therapy program). By purchasing a book you can add to that support. Go to www.WhoRescuedWho.mx and click on "Our Stuff" to find out where they are sold.